The Mummy Snatcher of Memphis

Natasha Narayan was born in India but emigrated to England at the age of five. She has had many jobs in journalism including working as a war correspondent in Bosnia. Like Kit Salter, Natasha loves travelling and exploring new places. She hopes to get to see some of the far flung deserts and mountains of her heroine – even if it's by bus rather than camel and yak. She lives in Oxford.

The Mummy Snatcher of Memphis

Natasha Narayan

Quercus

First published in Great Britain in 2009
This paperback edition published in 2010 by

Quercus
21 Bloomsbury Square
London
WC1A 2NS

A CIP catalogue reference for this book is available
from the British Library

ISBN 978 1 84916 021 6

10 9 8 7 6 5 4 3 2 1

Designed and typeset by Rook Books, London
Printed and bound in Great Britain by Clays Ltd, St Ives plc

❧ The Mummy Snatcher of Memphis ❧

For Nina with love

Mediterranean Sea

Siwa

Temple

EGYPT

❧ Part One ❧

Whatever happens follow your heart and your
conscience.
Maxim 11, *The Wisdom of Ptah Hotep*

The Wisdom of Ptah Hotep was discovered in Thebes,
Egypt by the Frenchman Prisse D'Avennes. The Papyrus
Prisse dates from the Egyptian Middle Kingdom (2500
BC) and is now displayed in the Louvre in Paris. The
oldest book in the world, this papyrus is a copy of an
even older work, one from the very dawn of Egyptian
history, over a thousand years before (3350 BC). This legendary work vanished long ago.

❧ Chapter One ❧

'Socks!'

My father, Professor Theodore Salter, stopped mid-stride and looked back at me in alarm. I jumped down our front steps and raced after him up the pavement.

'My dear?'

'Oh, Papa, you've gone and done it again!'

He looked at me, bewildered.

'Please examine your feet.'

'What's wrong with them?'

'You've forgotten your socks,' I explained. 'Don't you remember the blisters last time? You could barely walk when you came back from the museum!'

My father glanced down. From the tip of his top hat to his neatly pressed trousers he looked the perfect gentleman; all except for his feet, bare inside his stiff leather shoes.

'Extraordinary!' he said, as if he was looking at someone else's feet. 'How on earth did that happen?'

Father stepped out of his shoes and retreated home

without a backward glance. He seemed even more in a daze than usual. Resigned to my role as his keeper, I picked up his shoes and followed him. Outside our front gate, he bumped into a lady in an enormous hat. Her Pekinese yapped, snapping at Father with its pointed teeth.

'Down, Bonaparte,' the lady barked, staring at Father as if he was a lunatic.

How, you are probably wondering, does a man forget to put on his socks? The answer is that my father is not like other men; his brain does not connect with his body. While his feet tread the streets of Oxford, his head is somewhere altogether different. Like as not, in the realm of dusty manuscripts and ancient languages.

'What would I do without you, Kit?' Father asked once he was safely indoors and I had fetched his socks.

I know what you would do without me, I thought. You'd go to the museum in your nightgown and slippers. But I held my tongue. My father is all I have in the world. He has raised me single-handedly since the death of my mother six years ago. However, I am twelve years old now, and sometimes I think the tables have turned. These days, I seem to be doing much more of the 'raising' than my poor, dear father.

You see, just because I love my father doesn't mean I am foolishly indulgent. If you want to know about ancient Egyptian sarcophagi or need a parchment translated from Coptic, there is no better man to consult in the entire Empire than my father. But you cannot trust him with the simplest errand. Ask him to buy a jar of jam and he is likely to return with a bag of kippers. Even among the absentminded dons of North Oxford, Professor Theodore Salter's behaviour often seems eccentric. I suppose what I am trying to tell you is that Father was born with twice the normal amount of brains, but only half the sense. Indeed sometimes I feel like a nanny to a singularly half-witted toddler.

Father's cheeks were flushed as he put on his shoes. His breathing was agitated.

'Is everything all right?' I asked.

'Just rather rushed this morning because of this business with your Aunt Hilda.'

'What business? Isn't Auntie in Egypt on her expedition?'

'That's just it. Haven't you seen the *Illustrated London News?* She's back and she's coming to the museum this morning.' Father thrust a newspaper at me. Dated 22 October 1872, the headline read:

FAMOUS EXPLORER DONATES MUMMY TO PITT MUSEUM

11

The famous lady explorer Hilda Salter arrived back in London from Egypt yesterday. Miss Salter, who discovered the pearl of the Panagar in Persia last year, has been a member of the expedition to the tombs of Memphis in the Nile Delta.

A twenty-man team has been exploring the pyramid complex, which is said to include the tomb of the great pharaoh Isesi. There have been reports that the team have discovered fabulous treasures, as well as making enormous scientific advances in the understanding of ancient Egypt.

Dr Howard Cartwright, who is leading the expedition, told a reporter from the *London Times*, via telegraph:

'Wonderful treasures here! Expect to find burial place of Isesi any day now. Huge advance for English archaeology!'

Miss Salter travelled back to these shores by one of Thomas Cook's modern excursion steamers, the *Maharani*. She is said to be bringing an Egyptian mummy back with her – which she has announced she will donate to Oxford's Pitt museum.

'Gosh. A real mummy,' I breathed, my mind aflutter with visions of sand dunes and hollow-eyed figures wrapped in yards of white linen. 'May I come with you,

Papa? Please, *please*.'

'I'm late. I will have to go by carriage,' my father grumbled. He was back outside gesturing to a passing cab. The horse pulling the rather shabby hansom carriage slowed to a stop and he climbed in. The horse was a mangy creature, it looked tired and half-starved. How cross it makes me when I see animals that have been poorly treated.

'I would give anything to come with you,' I begged.

'Not now,' Father said. 'Ah! There's Madame Minchin. It's time for your lessons.'

Sullenly I let my governess in. She glanced at Father, with rather too wide a smile, but he failed to notice. This wasn't justice! Mummies and Egyptian treasure arriving at the museum and here I was stuck at home with the boring Minchin. How I hate being 'a *child*'. I am considered old enough to do most of the practical organising around the house. I am the one who makes decisions about menus and gives our housekeeper instructions. But when it comes to anything interesting – well, it seems I am a mere babe once again.

'Morning, Kathleen.' The Minchin swept in, her huge bustle buffeting me in the chest. No one but my governess calls me Kathleen. I sometimes think she does it because she knows how much I loathe the name. 'Please assist me by proceeding to the nursery and setting out

13

your books.'

The nursery is near the top of our steep house. It is a bright and airy room, covered with fading wallpaper and furnished with desks and a blackboard. In the corner stands my gold and maroon rocking horse. When I was little I called her 'Amelia' and loved to play with her. Lately she has been sorely neglected. I sat down at my place by the window. Soon there was a patter of feet on the stairs.

It was Rachel Ani, my closest friend. She is slightly older than me; with her halo of dark curls and rosebud lips, she is softly pretty. When I am impatient, Rachel is kind. Sometimes she can be sensible to a tiresome extent – but she tells me that I am fortunate to have her. Without her to keep me in order, she says, I would get into no end of scrapes. There was no sign of her brother Isaac – as usual he was dawdling in the street. The Anis are orphans, looked after by a guardian who is nearly as absentminded as my father. Isaac is just a year younger than Rachel, but he seems a puppy compared with my friend. He is always fiddling away with bolts and pieces of wire and fancies himself an engineer like the great Brunel. I do not take his whims seriously. No matter that boys are considered far superior to us girls, I still maintain they are silly creatures!

The Minchin was fussing away with her books,

smelling salts and glass of water when Isaac burst in. He streaked over the floor at terrific speed and crashed into her desk, knocking over a glass of water. The pool of water spread over the desk, narrowly missing Minchin's lap. 'Good gracious me!' She jumped up in horror. 'Whatever next?'

'Sorry,' Isaac gasped.

Trying to suppress my giggles I stared at Isaac's feet in astonishment. 'What on . . .'

'Do you like them?' he exclaimed. 'My latest invention! RollerShoes.'

'RollerShoes?'

'I've attached these to the soles of my boots.' Balancing on a desk with one hand, Isaac lifted a foot so I could see the tiny wheels glittering in the soles. 'You can go like the wind in RollerShoes. They're going to make me rich!'

I thought the RollerShoes looked fantastic but Rachel was obviously mortified. 'They'll never catch on,' she hissed at her brother. 'Take them off.'

'At once,' the Minchin added. 'Sit down, Isaac, and get out your copybooks. I shall have to have words with your guardian about your wild behaviour.'

A minute later Waldo Bell made a grand entrance, clumping in with a great deal of noise. He is an American and, without a doubt, the most annoying person I have ever met. Waldo had to leave his last school for mysterious reasons. Now he shares lessons with Rachel, Isaac and me, whom he persists in calling 'children'. One year older than us girls and he acts like our great-uncle. Certain people might think Waldo handsome, with his blond curls and pale blue eyes. He certainly has a high opinion of his own looks! For myself, I think arrogance is his chief quality.

The Minchin sat down, surveying us in a bored way. 'Attention, little scholars,' she said. 'This morning I think the boys can work on their Latin verbs. Rachel and Kathleen, we'll be doing a special session on etiquette. We're all aware that Kathleen's manners in particular could benefit from some serious attention.'

I was foolish enough to sigh. The Minchin glared at me, her eyes as hard as the shell of the black beetles that scuttle under our skirting boards.

'If you have no objection, Kathleen.'

I couldn't stop myself: 'I see no point in etiquette,' I burst out. 'It's a useless subject.' Waldo was looking at me and sniggering but I couldn't stop myself from steaming on. 'Why not Latin?'

The Minchin snapped. 'If you dream, as every young girl must, of being presented at court –'

'I would wake up screaming as from the foulest nightmare,' I interrupted.

16

Even Rachel, who would never attend a London season because she is Jewish, looked scandalised. The Minchin drew in her breath: 'How do you intend to find a husband if you're not a debutante, young lady? Or I suppose any chimney sweep will do!'

'I don't want to get married. Why should I have some man telling me what to do!'

'You should be so lucky,' Waldo whispered to me quietly, so our governess wouldn't hear. 'No one wants a bluestocking like you. You'll end up a hairy old spinster.'

'Better that than a fathead like you!' I flashed back. I knew it was a lame reply but it was all I could think of on the spur of the moment. This was a sore subject with me. Perhaps because my mother is dead, father is keen for me to learn 'the gentle arts'. But I do not intend to spend my life tightening my corset and waiting for some fool to ask me to dance. I said more calmly, 'As you all know, I'm interested in words. I intend to study languages, ancient languages and cultures. Perhaps when I'm older I'll be an explorer like my aunt or –'

'Enough!' The Minchin cut me off.

For a moment the room was so silent you could hear the doves cooing in the chimneys. The Minchin drew her thin lips together till they almost vanished into her chin. She took out the boys' Latin Grammars and distributed them, clacking round the wood floor with her sharp heels. Each clack was a note of disapproval.

With a sharp slap, the Minchin opened *Our Deportment* by a Mr Jeffrey Young. A foolish book, lent to us by Waldo's mother. Waldo's mother fondly believes her son to be a 'perfect little gentleman', but she was obviously less impressed by my manners.

I began to read:

General Rules of the Table

Refrain from making a noise when eating, or supping from a spoon and smacking the lips or breathing heavily when masticating food, as they are the marks of ill-breeding.

My mind wandered as it often does in the Minchin's lessons and I began making lists:

Things I Love:

– Adventure.
– Cantering around on my mare Jesse.
– Pyramids
– Treacle Tart and ices and barley sugar and butter scotch and caramel.

Things I hate:

– Learning 'manners'.
– Corsets.
– Boys who think they are better than girls.
– Cheese.
– The Minchin, the Minchin, the Minchin.

Oh why couldn't my tiresome governess just disappear in a puff of smoke, leaving me gloriously free? There was a thrilling account of my aunt's travels in the *Illustrated London News*. I'd pored over the engravings of strange tombs. The stories of pyramids and camels wandering the desert sands. The Minchin's bleating voice broke into my daydreams:

'I'm feeling a little faint, children. I think I'll just go upstairs for a moment and lie down. Pray continue with your work.'

The Minchin did look alarmingly pale, her skin milk-white next to her dark ringlets. She swept out of the nursery. I heard her heels on the stairs, clopping to the day-room where she took her rest. This was an answer to my prayers! We could hope for at least an hour without her interference. When the Minchin had one of her 'dizzy spells' she tended to disappear. I had my suspicions about how genuine her 'spells' were. Once when I went up to ask her a question she quickly hid something under the bedclothes. Not before I could make out the title in bold colours: *Lady Audley's Secret*. This is one of the books my father despises, trashy stories full of murder and romance. Personally I think they look rather exciting.

Not that I give a fig about the Minchin. This was our chance!

I hastily put my copybooks away and went to the door. 'I'm off out,' I said. 'Who's with me?'

Instantly there was uproar, everyone talking at once. I explained about the mummy arriving at the museum. I was going! I did not intend to miss this opportunity! Isaac was instantly up for the adventure and to my surprise so was Waldo. Only Rachel hung back.

'We'll get into awful trouble,' she said. 'Miss Minchin will be furious if she gets back and we're not here.'

'Oh, don't be such a namby-pamby.'

'We'll get a thousand lines.'

'It'll be worth every one,' I called back, taking the stairs two at a time. The others followed me. Reluctantly, not wanting to be left behind by herself, Rachel brought up the rear.

'I don't like this,' Rachel warned. 'Don't blame me when it all goes wrong.'

Poor Rachel. Of course no one was listening.

❧ Chapter Two ❧

We arrived at the Natural History Museum to find a commotion. A bustle of carriages, whinnying horses, dark foreigners dressed in shawls and loose white tunics, porters carrying huge boxes and yelling as they bumped into each other. Aunt Hilda was always a human whirl-wind; this chaos meant she could not be far away. I waded into the thick of the action, receiving an elbow in my face for my pains. Then I heard a familiar barking voice:

'Look sharp, boy. I haven't got all day.'

Aunt Hilda's stocky figure emerged out of the scrum. Her face was bronzed and weather-beaten, her hair dishevelled. But it was her clothes that made me stare in astonishment. She had cast off her skirt and was wear-ing trousers, of all scandalous things. At first I thought she was disguised as a man! Then I realised she was dressed in an odd sort of riding habit. Her jodhpurs were made of blue serge, which she had tucked into stumpy shoes. Shoes that would look clumsy even on my father.

My aunt would never cease to amaze me.

'It's not a sack of turnips, you ignorant clot,' Aunt Hilda boomed at a porter weighed down by a packing case the size of a large coffin. 'I haven't travelled all the way from Memphis with the Pharaoh's treasures, only to see it smashed to smithereens by a careless boy!'

The 'boy' in question was a middle-aged man with nut-brown skin. He was made even more clumsy by Aunt Hilda's barking and I feared he would drop the box altogether. Behind Aunt Hilda, like a jerky puppet, danced my father. This was a tremendous day for him. His face clearly displayed the agonies he was going through.

I shoved my way through the onlookers, the others hard on my heels.

'Kit? Are you not with Miss Minchin?' my father asked, seeing us appear through the crowd.

'You asked us to assist you,' I bluffed, knowing my father would not remember.

'Splendid,' he said vaguely, his eyes darting off towards a porter unloading a case from a large cart.

Aunt Hilda gave off berating the 'boy' with the packing case. She noticed me and strode over to give me a brisk hug.

'Can we help?' I asked.

'Got a pack of friends with you? Might as well make yourselves useful, I suppose. Give Abdul here a hand. I pay him ten shillings a month to drop my most prized possessions. Daylight robbery!'

I thought poor Abdul was doing a very good job, considering the size of the case, but I knew my aunt was a most demanding person. We all slotted in around Abdul and carefully carried the box into the museum. To reach the Pitt Collection we had to go through the arched hall of the Natural History Museum. Glass and steel soared above us. We marched past cases containing prehistoric bones and butterflies entombed in clear glass. Isaac loves the Natural History Museum. Declares it is the best in the world. For myself, I love the Pitt – or 'The Hole', as some call it. My father is the Director of this delightful collection of curiosities. Though the galleries in which the Pitt is housed are dark and fusty, it is a den of higgledy-piggledy delights. You may find everything of wonder there from shrunken witches' heads to towering totem poles.

Other porters followed us, laden down with even larger cases and trunks. Soon we were in the ante-room to the Pitt Collection and father was hopping around excitedly telling us to please, please be careful as we set down our goods. There were so many packing cases, corded with stout ropes and labelled FRAGILE in large letters. They filled the whole room.

'So, Theo. Have you made a plan?' Aunt Hilda asked.

'A plan?'

'Where do you intend to unpack?' she gestured around impatiently at the trunks and packing cases. 'I want to see my treasures have arrived safely. Also I'm expecting a chappie from the *Illustrated London News*. I expect they'll have an artist along to do an engraving of me with the mummy. They usually do.'

'How exciting.'

'Actually it's a rightful bore, but there it is. The public can't get enough of me, it seems.'

'We've cleared out a room. Would you like to inspect it?'

'I'd better. Make sure there is no damage from sunlight or dust. My collection is really rather special, Theo. I want it properly treated.'

Aunt Hilda ordered the porters to go outside into the yard and wait for the next delivery. Then she disappeared along with Father down a passage. The four of us were left alone with the mummy!

'I wonder,' I said, slowly wandering through the packing cases, 'which of these boxes is the mummy?' They bore the scuff marks and dust of their long journey from the East. They had travelled thousands of miles, swaying on the backs of camels, carried on the strong shoulders of native porters, by steamship and by carriage. Who knew what mysteries they contained?

'It will be a large rectangular box,' Waldo proclaimed. 'I expect this is the fellow.' He had halted by a case illuminated by a chance shaft of sunlight. Waldo laid a possessive hand on the box, as if he owned it himself. His blue eyes glowed with pride. The case was covered in tattered brown paper and twine and had a faded label on it. We all clustered round.

'What if it's cursed?' Rachel asked.

'Mummies are said to bring bad luck to those who defile their tombs,' Waldo said. 'Your aunt better watch out.'

'Whooo. The curse of the mummy.' Isaac danced around the box making sinister noises.

'Shush,' I said. 'This is a serious, scientific museum. If you're going to be silly, please leave.'

Taking no notice of me, Isaac went on with his idiotic noises.

'Quiet,' I said, more sternly and Isaac stopped.

'Worse than the Minchin,' he grumbled.

There was a moment's deep silence, broken only by the faraway rumble of hooves and wheels. Then, quite unmistakably, there was a groan.

A hoarse groan coming from within the room. I

turned on Isaac.

'Outside! This isn't the time for your pranks.'

'Wasn't me.'

Another groan, even louder, accompanied by a sharp crack. It couldn't have been Isaac, unless he had learned ventriloquism.

'The mummy!' Rachel gasped, clutching on to me.

The noise had come from the largest packing case in the room, placed upright against the wall. A dull brown in colour, it was the size of a big wardrobe. Was it my imagination or had it wobbled oh-so-slightly?

A chill spread through the room. The decaying breath of a spirit which had been dead for many thousands of years. An unreasoning fear took hold of me – and the others seemed to feel it as well, because for a moment we were all still as statues. Then I took hold of myself. I couldn't calm my too rapid heartbeat but I could move my feet. I went towards the box, while poor Rachel tried to hold me back.

Again that awful noise. A groan. This time, there was no doubt it was coming from inside the box.

❧ Chapter Three ❧

The packing case shivered. One side of the wood bulged slightly, as if something on the inside had fallen against it.

Rachel screamed.

'Hush!' I snapped.

Waldo murmured something to Rachel to calm her. But I noticed he did not move closer to the box to help me. There's boys for you, all very well with empty talk. Real courage is another matter.

I put out my hand to touch the case and again a tremor ran through it. There was something living inside.

'The m . . . m . . . mummy's awake,' Rachel stuttered.

'Small animal most like. A rat or some other rodent,' I said, to calm her down.

I noticed something strange. Like the other cases this one was corded with stout green twine. But somehow the twine had been frayed and broken.

There was only one way to find out. I ripped off the remnants of the twine and pulled the string off the box. The others crowded round to help me. Then, my hand trembling a little, I opened the lid. It wasn't at all difficult. The lid was loose, hardly difficult to prise off at all, despite its size and weight.

It was dark inside the box. A glimpse of golden paint, shining off the sarcophagus, the wood coffin that housed the ancient skeleton. The famous mummy! Then I noticed something dark and crouching. The whites of two eyes were visible, peering through the gloom.

'There's something in here,' I said. 'A trapped creature.'

Praying that whatever it was wouldn't bite me, I put my hand in the box. Instantly the thing sprang up, brushing my arm as it flailed out of the case. I had a confused impression of tattered garments and brown skin and then it was gone. Out of the box, scampering past me.

'Quick. Catch him!' Waldo shouted to Isaac.

Now I saw it was a skinny young boy, covered only in a ragged nightshirt. Waldo lunged at him, but the boy was too quick. He slipped past and was nearly at the door which led into the Natural History Museum. Isaac put his foot out, tripping the boy. He fell face downwards on to the floor and lay there, quite still.

'Don't hurt him,' I commanded Isaac, running over.

I knelt down next to him. While the others crowded around, I attempted to roll him over. The boy was covered in dust and filth from the packing case. Staring at me with tormented eyes, he looked like a wild creature, a desert fox perhaps. But I noticed that his nose and lips were finely modelled, his eyes large and lustrous and his eyelashes feathery. He was almost pretty – more like a girl than a lad.

'What is your name?' I enquired gently.

Numbly he looked at us, four heads hovering over him as he lay prone, cutting off his air and light.

'Don't be afraid. We're your friends.'

Waldo put his hand down and before I could stop him had given the boy a good pinch.

'Stop playing games,' he said roughly. 'What are you up to? Trying to steal the mummy's treasures?'

'Enough,' I snapped at Waldo, warding off more pinches. 'Can't you see how terrified he is?'

The boy was trembling, his dark eyes looking frantically around for escape. I laid a careful hand on his arm. I don't know what I said, mere soothing sounds really, but they seemed to calm him. Rachel, with her soft heart, had put her arm round his shoulder to lift him up. It was her actions, more than anything else, which comforted the creature. No one who looked into Rachel's warm face could suspect her of anything but kindness.

'Let's see if he has a knife,' suggested Waldo.

'He might want to stab us,' said Isaac.

Waldo began scrabbling around the boy looking for weapons. More foolishness! Of course there was nothing.

'Tell us your name,' I said.

Those large brown eyes only flickered around the room, like an animal. I was beginning to think the boy was a mute.

'It's impossible!' I said. 'He can't understand a thing.'

Rachel gave me a quick look, as if to chide me for my impatience. She looked into the boy's eyes, forcing him to look back at her and calm down. She pointed at me: 'Kit,' she said, very slowly and clearly. Then she did the same with all the others finally finishing off with herself: 'Me, Rachel.'

Finally an expression on that blank face. A small smile broke through his glumness, showing dazzling white teeth: 'Me, Ahmed.'

'Friends,' Rachel said.

'Friends,' the boy repeated.

'Ask him why he was hiding in King Isesi's case,' Waldo butted in.

'He might be a thief,' said Isaac.

'More like a spy. A rotten Frenchie spy,' Waldo said.

'Not a very good one,' I pointed out sarcastically. 'Any

longer in that packing case, I expect he would have dropped dead.'

While the rest of us were arguing Rachel had disappeared. She returned with a glass of water which she offered to Ahmed. He took it eagerly and downed it in three huge gulps.

'Food,' Rachel said. 'He needs food.'

A plan was beginning to form in my mind. I would smuggle Ahmed into our home. We would feed him, find him some decent clothes. Then, with Rachel's patient help we would try to find out his story. He looked no older than us, twelve or thirteen at the most. How did this poor creature come to be in Oxford, shivering even in a warm autumn? How did he wash up, hungry, ragged, frightened and alone, thousands of miles from his desert home?

I had already assumed, you see, that he was Egyptian. Those ebony eyes, the lack of English, the fact he was in the mummy case. That was our first clue. We had an Egyptian stowaway on our hands.

'We will find him some bread and cheese,' I said. 'We will take him home and feed him.'

Just then we heard Aunt Hilda's stentorian voice approaching down the corridor. 'Your arrangements are adequate, Theo,' she was saying. 'Adequate at best.'

'Thank you, my dear.'

'Less of the thank-yous. Could Do Better, that's what you need to tell yourself. Anyway, I suggest you call it the Hilda Salter Bequest. The very least you can do. A magnificent collection of Egyptology, even if I say so myself.'

'It's very fine indeed,' my father bleated.

Aunt Hilda had such a vibrant personality, she could force the strongest man into submission. Sadly Father was not the strongest man. For as long as he could recall, Papa had been terrified of his elder sister.

But the effect on Ahmed of Aunt Hilda's voice was extraordinary. He stood up, quivering. Then he bolted, crashing painfully into a large case. Without a murmur he got up and set off again.

'Quick, catch him!' Waldo ran after Ahmed.

By luck Ahmed had blundered into the dark corner of the room which led to my father's office. We caught him there and opening the door ushered him into Papa's sanctum, a crowded room, packed with cases, pottery, parchments and fragments of ancient bones. There were plenty of nooks and crannies in here where a skinny boy could remain undetected.

'It's all right,' I said. 'You'll be safe here. You can hide.'

That was one word Ahmed understood. He looked at me with huge, scared eyes. 'Hide,' he repeated. 'Hide.'

❧ Chapter Four ❧

Ahmed crouched in the corner, in the dark space between the edge of my father's desk and a bookshelf. More porters had entered the room next door, judging by all the banging and scraping coming through the wall. My aunt was busy being in charge, my father hard at work following orders.

The Egyptian boy was over his fit of terror. Still, there was something about his frozen stance that was unnerving. Surely such fear was out of all proportion? Aunt Hilda can be something of a dragon, granted. But she is not a mean-spirited person. Under her bristly exterior, I am convinced, lies a decent heart. The boy reacted to her voice as if she was the devil himself.

After some time, the banging outside ceased. Aunt Hilda and father had obviously found some new distraction. We heard their footsteps move away. Ahmed flopped and lay in a heap, quite still. We looked at each other and I shrugged. I didn't know what to do with him. It was Rachel who went over and knelt down.

'Ahmed,' she whispered.

'Rachel.'

'Everything will be all right, Ahmed.' The words were mere sounds to Ahmed. It was the soothing tone that comforted him. 'Nothing bad will happen to you. Please, you must trust us.'

'Bad.'

'No Ahmed. We are good! No harm will come to you.'

Ahmed uncurled a little. His eyes flickered to Rachel and then over all of us in turn.

Some calculation was going on in that tousled head. I could see it clearly in Ahmed's eyes. His skinny hands delved into the rags on his body and came out clasping a packet sealed in mustard-coloured wax paper. The packet was roughly three inches square with a hole at the top. A red cord was threaded through the hole. Ahmed, we now saw, wore the packet dangling from a cord around his neck.

'Rachel,' he said. He took a piece of parchment out of the packet and handed it to my friend.

Rachel took the roll of parchment and turned it over in her hands, almost stroking the rough surface. The wax paper was dusty and dirty, as you would expect, since it had travelled with Ahmed across half the world.

Inscribed around it in green ink were three symbols. I knew what they were: hieroglyphics! The mysterious language of the ancient Egyptians.

I knew what the symbols were called, but alas I could not read them. Right then and there I decided to learn hieroglyphics, so I could decode their secret.

Sensitivity is one of Rachel's finest qualities. She saw my eager face, knew that I was itching to get my hands on the packet. 'Kit,' she explained to Ahmed and offered it to me.

I unrolled it carefully. Inscribed on the top were the same three figures that were scrawled on the outside of the parchment. But underneath, to my great surprise, I saw there was writing I could understand. It was English, written in a fine, flowing hand. The others gathered round and I began to read it out:

These are the words of a dying man.

My name is Mustapha El Kassul. The boy who bears this letter is my son Ahmed Bin Mustapha El Kassul.

I live with my family in a small village by the blue waters of the Nile, near Memphis. In the Old Kingdom of the pharaohs it was capital of the greatest empire in the world. Such wealth! Mighty pyramids hewn from stone, monuments glittering with gold, surrounded by sparkling, white walls! Alas, Wealth crumbles to dust. These days we live simply, tilling our crops and tending our animals. Life has been good to us.

Something about the letter struck me as wrong. I stopped reading and looked at Ahmed. He was watching me warily. I was struck by his large, bright eyes. They were not the eyes of a hunted animal, as I'd thought earlier. They were far too intelligent. Almost – though I knew it was impossible – as if he could understand what I was reading.

'Your father writes very good English,' I said.

Ahmed looked to Rachel for help.

'Your father. He has very good handwriting.' I mimed holding a pen and writing on paper.

'Ah!' Illumination spread over the Egyptian's face and he uttered a word that I didn't understand.

Rachel who was watching him carefully, explained: 'I think he's trying to say scribe. Maybe someone else wrote it, like a village scribe.'

'They used to have village scribes over here. In the olden days when no one could read,' said Isaac. 'Perhaps the peasants in Egypt have scribes to write their letters because no one can read over there.'

I glanced back at Ahmed. His eyes were black as bee-

36

tles, glittering and impenetrable. 'Scribe, scribe,' he said several times, nodding his head. I went back to reading.

Our good fortune was about to change — all because of my very own nephew, Ali.

One night Ali failed to return for dinner. We feared for his life. I went out with a search party. To my horror I found the secret burial place of Ptah Hotep — vizier to the great Pharaoh Isesi of the fifth dynasty — had been defiled. The door was wrenched off, and a foul stench came from within. Someone had dropped a dead donkey into the shaft hoping the stink would discourage investigation. Thieves had been through the tomb like a pack of jackals — plundering, smashing — in their lust for treasure.

My head knew it was Ali — though my heart refused to believe it. He had been asking questions about the secret tomb and I had finally shown him where it was hidden.

Worse was to come. The heart scarab that lay in Ptah Hotep's bandages had gone! Worthless to all but us humble villagers whom it has protected down the flow of time. Legend has it that if the heart scarab leaves Memphis, tragedy will fall upon the village.

The shame of it smote me. I fell to the earth, pain piercing me. From that day on I have been a marked man living under a suspended sentence of death.

Our village is cursed.

Crops failed, goats strayed, milk turned sour. The priest tells me that our family has brought evil. The only way to end the curse is to find Ptah Hotep's scarab – the resting place of his Ba – his very soul – and bury it once more in his tomb.

You are welcome to all other treasures – but please let the man's soul rest in peace.

Mustapha El Kassul

p.s. Ptah Hotep's coffin is richly gilt with gold and turquoise. On it is inscribed his name in the ancient script and the figures of Anubis, the jackal-headed one, Maat, feathered goddess of truth and Ptah creator of all. The malachite heart scarab is buried under the linen bandages of his mummy.

We looked at each other, bewildered.

'What's a scarab?' Waldo asked.

'A kind of Egyptian beetle,' Isaac replied

Rachel hadn't been paying attention. 'We must help Ahmed,' she burst out.

'Ye-es,' I agreed, but I was troubled. I was thinking over the story. I liked Ahmed. He had an honest face and there was something winning about his manner. I was disposed to trust him. Could we? Was it true that the scarab's loss had smote down his father and cursed his village?

'We must, Kit,' Rachel repeated.

Ahmed was staring at me, as if trying to winkle into my mind. Wordlessly, his eyes begged for my help. He looked so forlorn. I made up my mind.

'We will do everything we can to find the scarab and restore it to Memphis,' I announced.

Rachel was overjoyed and hope flamed on Ahmed's face. Only Waldo looked dubious. 'Are you going to just take a native's word for this?' he demanded.

'Why ever not?'

'Well . . . he's a native!'

'So?'

'Natives are more likely to lie and cheat. They're like children. They don't know the difference between right and wrong.'

'All the children I know understand the difference between right and wrong perfectly. Of course it may be different in America.'

'He's probably after the mummy's treasure. Natives are just born greedy!'

'For goodness' sake . . .' I said and stopped, spluttering. Waldo's attitude disgusted me, though I myself had felt a stab of caution at Ahmed's story. It is contrary of me I know, but when Waldo becomes all superior I can't help taking the very opposite point of view. I hate it when people look down on other races: folk whom they have never even met! I was, however, struggling to put my feelings into words when Rachel spoke in her quiet way.

'People say the same thing about Jews. They say we're born greedy.'

Waldo blushed. 'I didn't mean anything of the sort –' he began when I cut in.

'Look at him! He's a poor, scared boy. Anyway, what treasure? We're not talking of precious gold. A mouldy old scarab!'

'It could be worth something.'

'Anyway, who has more right to it, Aunt Hilda, or the villagers?'

Waldo had the decency to look a little less sure of himself.

'We've got to help him,' I announced. 'We've got to fight for justice.'

Put like that even hoity-toity Waldo agreed. We would steal the scarab! Though it could scarcely be called theft to snatch it in order to return it to its rightful owners. Once we had the scarab, we would somehow find Ahmed safe passage on a steamer back to Egypt.

How the best intentions can come undone! In our foolish hope, we imagined that righting Ahmed's wrongs would be a simple matter. We are English, we thought, citizens of Queen Victoria – and children of the greatest empire the world has ever known. Our soldiers have conquered a tremendous portion of the globe – so vast 'the sun never sets on the British Empire'. What use is our power if it is not tempered with mercy?

Besides, in my secret heart I thought, how hard can it be to help a simple Egyptian boy? I imagined it would be short work to sneak off with the scarab. After all, my father trusted me in the museum.

Sadly, it didn't go quite according to plan. Over the next few weeks we experienced terror like never before – and came face to face with pure wickedness. All of us were to be sorely tested. As for your friend, Kit Salter, I was to face the hardest lesson of all. I learned that I am not *always* right. (Only, I will concede, 99 per cent of the time.)

❧ Chapter Five ❧

'It is a pleasure to make your acquaintance again, sir,' Papa said to Ahmed, between forkfuls of pheasant casserole. 'I believe we met at the Royal Geographic Society last week.'

I glared at Father. Surely even he could see that Ahmed was a boy and not one of his learned professors? Of course Father treats *everyone* exactly the same. Last week I found him asking the lad who comes around to sharpen the kitchen knives his opinion of the best system for reading hieroglyphics. Poor Ahmed was looking at Papa blankly. All the way through the first course – a rather watery turtle soup – Papa had utterly failed to notice him, even though the Egyptian was seated to his left. Ahmed must have thought he'd escaped his notice.

'Do forgive me, sir. I believe I've been foolish enough to forget your name,' my father tried again.

'I . . . is,' Ahmed stuttered.

Ahmed, it turned out, could understand a few words

of English, as long as one spoke very slowly and clearly. But Father's courtesy was beyond him. The boy turned frantically to me for help. Luckily I was ready with a white lie:

'Surely you remember Ahmed, Papa? Aunt Hilda asked us to give him lodging for a few weeks?'

Papa's brow cleared. 'Of course. Silly of me.'

Leaning a little over the table, I dropped my voice to a whisper. 'You will have to be very patient with Ahmed; he speaks scarcely a word of English.' I was going to go on, with some nonsense about how Ahmed's father was an expert on the pyramids, when I decided to stop. There was always a danger that if something actually interested Papa he would remember it.

Ahmed was opposite me, his face partly hidden by our soup tureen. The half I could see shone with cleanliness. He was dressed in one of Isaac's white shirts, which hung loosely on his skinny frame. We had given him a hot bath, as soon as we had smuggled him back from the museum, helping Dora the housemaid haul up steaming tubs of water. Ahmed's tattered old clothes had gone straight into the rubbish heap. He had been scrubbed and polished to within an inch of his life. He seemed a new boy, smart and clean, the very pinnacle of respectability.

Rachel and Isaac were having dinner with us this

evening. It helped greatly that Rachel was sitting next to Ahmed. How he adored her. He had attached himself to my kind friend like a lost puppy. His eyes followed her everywhere. Without her, he felt extremely anxious.

After the pheasant stew came the highlight of the evening, a thick, rich, creamy trifle of stupendous gorgeousness. Layers of sponge, soaked in rich marsala wine, covered in jam and whipped cream. Ahmed had not eaten much of the savoury courses. The Minchin would have considered his manners even worse than mine. He had started to eat his meat with his knife, till I gave him a kick under the table. Ahmed had looked as though he was eating sawdust with the main course. When the pudding arrived he had taken one tentative taste. Clearly he had low hopes of English cooking; it must have tasted sadly bland beside the spicy food of his homeland. But I'm glad to say that the trifle redeemed our national fare. It took but a nibble for a look of rapture to spread across his face. He gobbled up his whole bowl, and accepted three more helpings.

Egyptian puddings are, obviously, not a patch on English ones!

Rachel, Isaac, father and I enjoyed the trifle just as much as Ahmed. We were finishing our extra helpings, feeling stuffed to the point of sickness, when the doorbell rang. A minute later Dora the housemaid appeared, all flustered.

'I tried telling her you were in the middle of dinner, sir,' Dora explained 'The lady wouldn't wait.'

'Out of my way, girl.' Aunt Hilda elbowed Dora aside. 'Theo, I have had an inspiration!'

'Er . . . very well, dear,' Papa bleated, while Dora, defeated, retreated back to the kitchen.

'A stroke of genius, some might call it.'

As soon as I saw her my heart began to pound. This could be awkward. Might she unmask Ahmed?

I needn't have worried. Aunt Hilda was so full of her latest idea she scarcely glanced at the rest of us. She had changed into a more ordinary dress, though she still wore her mannish shoes and was lugging a large sack-cloth bag. Clumping on the wooden floor, she strode up and began talking, banging on the table to emphasise her words.

'This will get Monsieur Champlon's goat! Why even the New York papers will sit up and take notice. I expect an international sensation!'

'What are you –' Father began but Hilda cut him off.

'You know how much interest my collection has caused. I've had *The Times*, the *Manchester Guardian* . . .' Aunt Hilda began ticking off newspapers on her fingers. 'Fully a dozen papers and magazines would like to attend the unveiling of the Hilda Salter Bequest. You know me,' Aunt Hilda embraced us all in her glance. 'I don't do half measures. I can't be bothered with mayors making tedious speeches. Let's treat the newspapers to something special, I thought. So I had my inspiration! It is a wonderful idea.'

'Ye-es,' Father said, dubiously.

Abruptly, Aunt Hilda noticed us: 'Not in front of the children, Theo.'

'Pardon?' Father asked.

'We will discuss this in private. I'm sorry, Kit, my dear, but this is a delicate matter. As they say, walls have ears. Come along, Theo.'

Father trotted along after Aunt Hilda, as she marched to the drawing room, slamming the door shut. 'I'll be back in a moment,' I whispered to the others and tiptoed after them. I stood outside, my ear pressed to the door. Unfortunately all I could hear was a dull murmur. I was just about to give up when suddenly, the voices rose.

'Theo!' Aunt Hilda barked.

'I *will not*,' my father's bleat came through the door.

'I can't have explained myself properly, Theo.'

'I won't change my mind.'

'That is your last word on the subject?'

'It is.'

There was the sound of stomping feet. In panic I pressed myself against the wall but Hilda didn't notice me as she flung the door open, though I was an inch away from her.

'I will have to take the Hilda Salter Bequest elsewhere,' she shouted at my father over her shoulder. 'The mummies will go tomorrow to a museum where they are properly appreciated.'

'So be it,' Father replied. 'You will *never* get me to change my mind.'

❧ Chapter Six ❧

'Why did I let Hilda persuade me to do this?' Father wailed. He was backstage at the museum, looking a little comical dressed up in a flowing costume as the Egyptian god Anubis. Of course poor Papa had given in to every single one of his sister's demands and now he was gazing at the audience assembling for his entrance. Such was his horror, he could have been watching his executioners gather, rather than a perfectly respectable Oxford crowd.

'You have to learn to stand up for yourself, Papa.'

'How? How am I to stand up for myself?'

'You must learn to say no.'

'I said no a thousand times.'

'Say it once and mean it. Let your NO be the end of the matter.'

Father wasn't listening.

'I am undone,' he moaned. He had recognised some-one in the crowd. My eyes followed his finger, which was pointing to a white-bearded old gentleman in the middle of the front row. The gentleman was accompanied by a lady in purple sateen, carrying a black parasol. They looked distinguished and, well, rather nice, if a bit grumpy.

'It is Charles Darwin, Kit. Oh, I am ruined.'

Poor, poor Father. The great naturalist was his hero. Mr Darwin's theory that men are descended from apes caused huge controversy, but Father reckoned him the 'greatest mind of the age' and was proud to count him a friend. It was wicked of Aunt Hilda to have invited Mr Darwin. Not to mention the newspapermen. What could I do to help Father? I was forced to put a brave face on it.

'Shush, Papa, think of the fabulous mummies aunt Hilda has brought you. The Pitt will have the finest collection in Europe!'

'For all my hard work to come to this. Mr Darwin is here! He will see me playing the lead role in a foolish pantomime.' An ancient Egyptian mask of the jackal god Anubis, covered in crackled gold, trembled in father's hands. 'I am a serious man, Kit. My reputation will be ruined. My museum will become a joke.'

'He will not recognise you when you put on the mask. Remember, Papa, do not take the mask off, whatever happens.'

I could not afford to pamper Father for too long. Waldo, Ahmed, Rachel and Isaac were waiting for me. This was our chance. We had to get to the mummy now before my aunt's great show began. With a reassuring squeeze of Father's arm, I slipped off into the wings where I hoped the coffin was kept. It was a badly lit, dusty space but there it was, lying on the floor. My heart began to beat as I saw the sarcophagus: a beautiful thing, covered in hieroglyphics and paintings of the ancient gods – Maat, feathered goddess of truth, Ptah, creator of all, Anubis, the jackal-headed one.

'Help me open it,' I hissed, straining to lift the heavy wooden lid. Waldo came up and assisted me. The wood gave a loud creak. We strained again and it gave another creak. It was going to be very difficult to open.

'Good heavens!' a voice rang out. Aunt Hilda stood in front of us, swathed in white robes that made her look like a rather hefty mummy. 'What on earth?' By her side stood two of her Egyptian workers.

'We were just curious,' I blurted. 'We wanted to see the mummy.'

'Out of the question. This sarcophagus has not been opened for *thousands of years*. *I* want to be the one to do it! Scoot now. We have to prepare for my grand mummy unwrapping.'

I was thoroughly annoyed with myself as we made

our way into the theatre. We had blown our chance to find the scarab. Of course, Aunt Hilda was planning to unwrap the mummy as part of the show. Why had I hung about listening to Father's moaning? As we shoved our way through the packed benches I cursed myself for not acting sooner. If they unravelled the mummy's bandages surely they would find the scarab and our task would become much harder?

No sooner had we found a place to stand in the corner than a blanket of darkness descended on the hall; so deep we became shadows against the velvet night. At the back of the hall a woman screamed. Somewhere a plaintive bell wailed. A strange smell swept through the room, musky and rich, redolent of desert tombs and rotting flesh. Rachel felt her way to me and gripped my arm in the darkness. The wailing grew and two yellowy gaslights flared at the front of the stage as the curtains slowly pulled back. Perched in all its splendour on a rough oak table was the coffin of Ptah Hotep. How its wonderful hieroglyphs shone, glowing turquoise, scarlet and gold. Those eerie paintings of ancient gods had come back to haunt modern man.

Two of Aunt Hilda's workers, dressed in pale robes, stood on each side of the coffin. They carried ancient Egyptian instruments called sistrums, which are a bit like babies' rattles. As they shook their sistrums, a gruesome figure emerged out of the murk. Pointed ears, a long doggy snout, red eyes gleaming out of the grotesque shadows of its face. A golden headdress flowed down its back. The jackal god, Anubis, lolloped to the front of the stage on his spindly legs. Around me I could hear the deliciously fearful *oooohs* and *aaaahs* of the ladies. Even though I knew it was dear papa under that mask, I shivered. This was something feral, an ancient and malicious beast.

'What is the life of a man, but a single heartbeat in the endless circle of time?' the voice, rasping out from behind the mask was hoarse and ugly, not like Father at all. 'What are your miserable pleasures? What are your pains? All will become dust under the merciless gaze of Ra the invincible.' The jackal held out a paw. In the sickly yellow light a fine stream fell to the floor, where it formed a small pyramid of powder.

'Observe the coffin of Ptah Hotep. Four thousand years ago he was high and mighty. As vizier to the great Pharaoh Isesi he ruled over the lives of all about him. Lords shook at his approach, fine ladies quailed at his shadow. Slaves leapt to his bidding.

'Now what is he? All his power has crumbled, his riches come to nought but a handful of sand. In the afterlife kings and viziers are nothing. In the world of the dead you answer to me, Anubis, guide to the underworld, judge of your sins.'

I could imagine this monster snuffling around in cemeteries, rooting out rotting corpses. It made me shudder. I would run a mile from such a thing. Poor Father, trapped inside that costume. Still, I must admit I was rather impressed with his performance. He had learnt his lines well.

'Hear me, Ptah Hotep, vizier to the great Pharaoh Isesi. Now I will raise thee from the d-d-dead,' the jackal intoned.

Sinister shadows raced across the white walls. The jackal leaned over the table, the tip of its snout hovering over the coffin, its hands spread wide. Silence descended on us, as every man, woman and child in the audience drew in their breath. As for me, I could scarce breathe at all. Rachel squeezed my hand and I must confess I took comfort from her touch. She was so warm, so real.

A stocky figure with the head of a stork-like bird appeared, elbowed the jackal aside and announced. 'I am Thoth, god of wisdom. I have come here to unroll the mummy.'

Thoth advanced towards us. I could see its ibis mask was not as ancient as that of Anubis. The beak was painted with fresh gold paint. Whereas the jackal was sinister, the stumpy figure of Thoth, with its nodding beak, was almost comical. Anyone less like a bird than my sturdy little aunt I could not imagine.

Thoth and Anubis, my aunt and my father, approached the wooden coffin and each took one side. There was a crack, a rending of aged wood, that echoed through the theatre. The lid came away in their hands, exposing something gleaming white underneath. The audience gasped. Some people so forgot themselves as to stand on their seats. Thoth and Anubis lifted the mummy out and the Egyptian 'boys' quickly approached to remove the coffin. Finally here it was, the ancient corpse in its swaddling of bandages, laid out on a table before our fascinated eyes.

Thoth waddled forward, rooted around under the mummy then emerged with an end of the bandage in its hand.

'STOP!' A voice yelled.

It was Father. He tore off his mask. 'Stop!' he howled again.

In my wilder flights of fancy I had imagined the mummy coming to life, slowly raising itself up on the stage and taking a few faltering steps towards the petrified crowd. But I never dreamed of this. My father, unmasked, advancing upon the corpse while a stream of frenzied jabber came out of his mouth, ripping apart the mummy's bandages with shaking claws.

Why was he behaving like a lunatic? Especially after I

had warned him against removing his mask.

Aunt Hilda tore off her own mask and advanced upon her brother with a brow like thunder: 'Theo! Have you gone stark, raving mad? We will have to admit you to Bedlam at this rate.'

My father turned to her, a tangle of bandages in each hand. 'Don't you see?'

'I see that you have let me down. Again.'

'The mummy's a fake.'

'A what?'

'A Fraud! A Fake! A Cheap Modern Copy!'

'Nonsense.'

'These bandages are new. I'll stake my life on it. They have never been anywhere near the desert!'

❧ Chapter Seven ❧

It took a second for my aunt to understand my father. Just another second to name the thief.

'Gaston!' she roared. 'That French blighter Gaston Champlon has stolen my mummy.'

'Control yourself,' Papa wailed. 'Please, Hilda, remember your, er . . . dignity.'

Pandemonium broke out among the audience. Several ladies fainted and had to be carried out into the fresh air to be dosed with smelling salts. Some of the younger men scurried to the aisles, as if offering to battle the French there and then. A few scholarly-looking old gentlemen were heard to enquire what all the fuss was about.

Aunt Hilda was spitting fury: 'Gaston has always been jealous of my Egyptian finds. He is a foul garlic-eating fiend.' She advanced to the front of the stage and shook her fist at imaginary Frenchmen in the audience. 'This means war, Champlon. I will hunt you down and I will make you pay. There is no hiding place from my vengeance.'

Poor Father was hanging on to his sister, trying to attract her attention. She shook him off her sleeve like an annoying ant. Father has several friends among the scholars of Paris. He is a man of peace not war. I know he would hate his sister to make trouble. Especially with Napoleon's war-mongering still a vivid memory.

'Come on,' I said to my friends. 'We'd better go back-stage. See if we can do anything to help Father.'

Ladies were swooning on the strong arms of their escorts. The confusion was indescribable as everyone fled in a different direction. Somehow my four friends and I managed to fight our way through the throng to the stage door. I opened it a crack, just enough to allow the others through. I shut the door firmly in the face of a man, with the rat-like look of a reporter from one of the scandal sheets.

Someone had lowered the curtain. I prayed the thick velvet would muffle my father and aunt's argument.

'You need evidence. You can't just accuse this man without evidence,' Father said.

'I *know* this is Gaston. I recognise the way he works.' Aunt Hilda took up her Thoth mask and smashed it to the floor in a fit of rage. 'He stole all the glory from me in Luxor!'

'If you're wrong he could set the lawyers on you. He would accuse you of spreading lies and injuring his reputation. You would have to pay huge sums of money in damages.'

Father need not have bothered. Aunt Hilda was not listening. A stream of furious – and not necessarily accurate – insults flew from her foam-flecked mouth: 'Foul frog. Horrendous Hun! Rotten rotter. He means to ruin me!'

I went up to the mummy itself. Only a blind man would have been fooled by the bandages. Why, they positively dazzled with starchy whiteness. No way could this mummy have been buried under the desert sands for thousands of years. I gave the bandages a firm yank. They came away easily. Soon I was holding a yard of linen and had exposed the so-called corpse.

It was nothing but a bundle of twigs. Common sticks wrapped in stout twine.

When she saw the 'corpse' Aunt Hilda grew pale. 'Gaston mocks me. He laughs at me in front of the world's newspapers.'

Something fluttered out of the wad of bandages in my hand and flew to the floor. I stooped and picked it up. For a moment I stared, puzzled, at the thing in my hands. No one else noticed it and so I did something very wrong. Something I hope you would never do. I put the fragment into my pocket.

The appearance of an Egyptian servant in our midst helped to distract attention from me. He was carrying a loaded platter. Steam rose enticingly out of a teapot.

'Cup of tea, Hilda?' Father begged. 'Tea is so very good for the nerves.'

'Nerves? Blast my nerves. Don't care a hoot for them. I want Gaston arrested. Want to see him pay!' But Aunt Hilda consented to sit down and have a cup.

Someone was knocking loudly on the stage door. A moment later a servant appeared followed by an old gentleman. When I saw the bushy beard my heart sank. How many more blows could father take? It was his idol, Charles Darwin.

'My humblest apologies, dear sir,' Father sloshed tea everywhere in his eagerness to rush to the famous scientist's side 'I would not have had you witness this tawdry farce. Not for anything!'

'Tawdry indeed,' Aunt Hilda snorted. 'It was a very refined production.'

'Do forgive me. It was a foolish and common –'

'Nonsense, Theo,' Mr Darwin smiled. 'I enjoyed it immensely.'

'What?'

'It was great fun!'

'Fun?' Father asked, as if he did not know the meaning of the word.

'I can't remember when I last enjoyed something so much. Emma said to me: "Charles," she said, "this is just the tonic you need for your nerves."' Mr Darwin patted my father kindly on the arm. 'Jolly good show.'

'It didn't go quite . . . according to plan.'

'Things rarely do, my dear fellow.'

Cheered by the relief on Father's face, I left the grown-ups to it and beckoned the others to follow me through the stage door to the emptying theatre. Chattering knots of people were still huddled in the ante-room. The fabulous canapés and glasses of champagne, which had been provided for the guests, were largely untouched. Waldo and Isaac grabbed a few prawns in aspic and I took a handful of cheese puffs. I shook off the same rat-faced newspaperman, who had recognised me as Professor Salter's daughter. Then we went outside to the front of the museum and sat down together on a park bench.

'So,' mused Waldo. 'It looks like the Frenchman stole the mummy. I wonder why.'

'I don't believe it,' I said.

'What do you know about it, Miss Clever-clogs?'

'I just don't think it was the Frenchman. Not unless he lives in the East End of London, and is a dab hand with the sewing needle.'

'What?' Waldo said rudely.

'Don't tease us, Kit,' Isaac put in. 'Tell us what you mean.'

'I have a clue.' I drew forth the thing that had fluttered out of the mummy's bandages. It was a grimy, water-stained bit of cloth.

'What on earth is *that*?' Waldo asked.

Rachel was studying the fragment curiously. 'What does it have to do with the mummy?'

'Can I have it?' Isaac asked.

Slightly reluctantly I handed it over and Isaac took it, turning it over this way and that. Finally a smile broke out on his face. 'You are clever, Kit,' he said.

'Thank you.'

'Stop making up mysteries,' Waldo grumbled.

'I'm not.'

'Course you are. Just to make yourself seem clever and important.'

'Hold on, Waldo.' I held up the greasy slip. 'This is a tailor's mark. You know one of the labels tailors sew into their clothes to identify their firm. Look, here are the initials of the tailor and here is the beginning of the letter S –'

'Capital S, and part of a small p for Spitalfields,' Isaac interrupted. 'I'm guessing that the mummy's bandages came from a tailor with the initials MZ.'

'And Spitalfields is where most of the London tailors

are based. The mummy' bandages must be scrap linen from one of the firms there,' I added. 'So all we have to do is find a tailor with the correct initials.'

Waldo couldn't help being impressed. He reddened slightly, annoyed at being shown up by a mere *girl*. 'There are probably dozens of tailors in Spitalfields with the initials MZ,' he muttered, but I took no notice. He was only trying to save face.

'I'm going east,' I announced.

'Can I come?' Isaac asked immediately.

Isaac can be relied on. He has sporting blood and is always up for a challenge.

As for the others, it was as if I had declared I was going to the moon, such is the fear of London's East End. I have heard that district is a den of wickedness. How I longed to see it! Rachel, tediously, was the most nervous. (Sometimes I wonder why I do not have a more adventurous friend.) She frowned at me, while Waldo turned up his nose in what he hoped was a manly way. All the while Ahmed was silent, clearly trying to follow our talk.

'Scared?' I smiled at Waldo. 'You don't have to come if you think it's too *dangerous*.'

'Hardly,' he answered coolly. 'I suppose I shall have to chaperone you. Someone will have to look after the *girls*.'

'I fear you will have a wasted trip. I intend to look after myself.'

❧ Part Two ❧

To listen is better than anything – thus perfect love is born.

Maxim 39, *The Wisdom of Ptah Hotep*

✺ Chapter Eight ✺

'Help!' I screamed. My boots had skidded on something foul on the pavement. I toppled and would have landed with my bottom in the slush if strong hands had not caught me under the elbows. I turned round to see who had saved my skirts from the slime. Oh no, it was as I feared.

'Thank you,' I muttered, checking under my boot. There was the skin of a jellied eel stuck to the sole. I removed it with a fingertip and flung it savagely away.

'My pleasure.' Waldo smirked. 'Always at your service, ladies.'

I wanted to say something biting, to wipe that horrid look off Waldo's face. Annoyingly, I could think of nothing on the spur of the moment.

'Are you all right, Kit?' Rachel fluttered around my elbow.

'Don't be uneasy on my account. Direct your attention to staying upright.'

'We should never have come here,' Rachel put her hand on my arm, while she stared around us fearfully.

Until this humiliation, everything had gone to plan. Yesterday I told Papa I wanted to go shopping in London's fashionable Regent Street. Distracted with mummy troubles he was glad to agree. He is always delighted when I take an interest in anything feminine. He had generously given me three whole guineas and we had agreed that Aunt Hilda would put us up for a few days at her house in Bloomsbury. However, instead of the glittering West End, the hansom carriage had deposited us in Petticoat Lane, in the darkest East. This, I guessed, was the centre of the tailoring district.

We were in the midst of a riot of foul and greasy tatters. Dress coats, frock coats, livery, plaids, knee breeches. Gentlemen's garments in every faded shade of black, brown and blue. The ladies' dresses: drab plum and violet, dingy maroon and green. Spilling into the sewage-gushing gutters were thousands of boots and shoes, shining and newly blacked. Look closer and you could see the split heels and worn soles. The rent and repaired leather. Tumbled over the boots were dribs and drabs of handkerchiefs and lace under-things; so washed and worn they would never be white again.

'I would never wear such rags.' I muttered.

Rachel looked at me reproachfully. 'Many people have no choice, Kit. They must either wear "such rags" or freeze to death.'

Instantly I felt ashamed. Why is Rachel always so right? She acts as if she has a personal telegraph line to the god of good hearts.

The lane seethed with a mass of ragged people. Now that Rachel had pointed it out, I could see that many, if not most, were dressed in the clothes for sale all around us. The women were tired and hollow-eyed, some with mewling babies perched on their hips or hanging by a strip of cloth from their shoulders. The men were lean, scarred with disease and fighting. Half-naked children played in the gutters. The stench of sewage, sweat, fried food and dirt seemed to swirl in foggy green air. I had never thought dirt had a smell before. It was so over-poweringly disgusting I wanted to put my handkerchief in front of my nose. For a moment I thought I might swoon, as if I was a feeble namby-pamby like the Minchin.

'This not London,' Ahmed said, looking around with a dazed expression. 'Where is?'

'Yes it is,' I replied. 'This is the East End of London.'

'London rich. Biggest city of Empire. Richest city of world.'

What Ahmed was saying was true. Of course London is the biggest and best city in the world. Right then and there I resolved to take him somewhere grand, Pall Mall or Regent's Park.

'This is more like bad place in Cairo. Very bad place.'

'We have poor people too,' Rachel explained.

I could see Ahmed wasn't really convinced. He must have been told stories about London, he probably thought the streets would be paved with guineas. In truth I shared a little of his shock. Never had I been so grateful for my cosy home in North Oxford. The golden spires, green fields and fresh air.

'Isaac! Isaac!' Suddenly Rachel was yelling. 'Isaac! Where are you?'

The boy had vanished. All around us were dirty bonnets, greasy toppers and foul bowler hats, without a sign of Isaac's brown curls. I felt out of my depth. Still, I had to be strong. I had dragged everyone here. This was my responsibility.

'He may be in the hands of those Skinners,' Rachel moaned. 'Oh Kit, this is *your* fault.'

We had heard the stories. 'Skinners' would lure children into alleyways with sweets and then strip them naked and make off with their clothes. Gangs of muscular 'garrotters' overpowered their victims in broad daylight!

Ahmed was pulling at my hand.

'Not now, Ahmed. We have to find Isaac.' I said, shortly.

'Please, you look, Kit – *see Isaac.*'

Ahmed was pointing down an alley even fouler than Petticoat Lane. A grubby signpost said Raven Row. A quarter of the way down was a beige and brown blur. I stared and it focused into Isaac, pausing without a care, on the edge of an excited crowd.

For a instant I hesitated, then taking a deep breath I took the plunge. All remnants of light and air were cut off in this foul lane. The soot-blackened houses lurched crazily inwards, as if they were drunk and about to fall down to the ground in a stupor. Through steamy gratings in the pavement I glimpsed the hovels below. Nine, ten, eleven men and women huddled together, stitching away as if their lives depended on it.

'What are you playing at!' Rachel scolded once we'd caught up with her little brother. 'It's dangerous round here. We must stick together.'

Isaac didn't trouble to answer. He pointed to the scene in front of him. A swarthy man with a knife scar down one side of his face had a white rat on his bare arm and a carrot in his mouth. As we watched, the rat ran up the arm, somersaulted, righted itself and then took the carrot out of its owner's mouth. The crowd cheered and a few coppers pattered into his hat.

'I wonder if I could make an invention of that,' he said excitedly. 'A mechanical rat, that plays tricks.'

'Come on, Isaac,' I said firmly, pulling him by the arm away from the crowd. 'We have detecting to do.'

Something had caught my eye further down the alley, a glint of a sign. 'ZWINGLER'S', it said in large letters.

The others followed me, past numerous sweatshops and small tailors, till we came to the shop in question. The entrance was crowded with military clothes, a welcome splash of scarlet in these drab surroundings. In smaller letters under the large wooden sign were the words: 'Moses Zwingler's, clothier and tailor to the Gentry. All garments stitched to highest standards.'

The shop was empty save for a thin girl of about nineteen years of age, with sallow skin, red-rimmed eyes and surprisingly abundant brown curls. Lovely curls, if they were brushed and cleaned. Indeed a little like Rachel's glorious ringlets.

The five of us picked over the clothes, looking for markings until Waldo called me over with a whistle.

'I found your clue for you, Miss Detective,' he said.

He had it! Inside a top hat was a tailor's mark, the first letters of which were identical to the scrap I had found in the mummy. For a moment it seemed as if Waldo would not let go of the hat. I wrested it from him and strode up to the shop girl, with the top hat in my hand.

70

'Where is your master?' I asked.

She stared at me blankly.

'We have a question for Moses Zwingler.'

Still those hollow brown eyes showed scarcely a flicker of intelligence. It was Ahmed who came to the rescue. Tugging at me he whispered: 'She no speak English.'

Of course, she must be foreign. From Russia, maybe, if the strange lettering on many of the garments was a clue.

'What shall we do?' I wondered. Unexpectedly, Rachel took over. Leaning forward she began muttering in some strange language, clearly surprising the shop girl. Rachel went on, leaning forward on the dirty shop counter and talking soft and low. After a few moments of this the girl answered a question. Then she began to chatter, very quickly.

'What are they talking about?' I asked Isaac.

'My sister is very good at Hebrew. Me, I'm useless. I hate synagogue.'

Of course, these shopkeepers must be Jewish.

'What's going on, Rachel?' I hissed. My friend and the shop girl were deep in conversation and seemed to have forgotten the rest of us altogether.

Rachel turned around. 'This is Sara Zwingler,' she explained. 'She is Mr Zwingler's niece. She remembers all about making the mummy. She asks us to follow her. Quick, her uncle will return soon.'

Sara padded over to the front and swiftly closed the shutters, then she beckoned us and we followed her through a narrow passage that smelled strongly of fish.

'Be quiet, for heaven's sake,' Rachel said, looking particularly hard at me. 'Sara's uncle will kill her if he finds out about this.'

We emerged into a poky room lit by three gas jets. Some twelve or thirteen men were sitting cross-legged on the floor, stitching 'slops' – the kind of clothes you buy ready-made. Around them were piles of cloth in every colour and fabric, not to mention pots, pans and personal things as well. The men were like living skeletons, you could see the patterns of their bones making a jigsaw under their skin. The lack of air, the hiss of gas, the bright lights made my nose block and eyes swell.

Sara muttered something to Rachel and my friend translated for us: 'These are "Greeners" – Jews fresh off the boat from Russia. They speak little or no English and have few skills. Sara says her uncle is kind. Better than many "sweaters". He makes his men work only sixteen hours a day – from six in the morning till ten in the night.'

Kind, I thought disbelievingly.

Meanwhile Sara was speaking to one of the men

whom she called Baruch: his hand froze, needle suspended in mid-air. He looked at me, Rachel, Waldo, Ahmed and Isaac and then back at Sara. It was as if he was taking account of us all. This man was younger than many of the others. He was handsome, with a long thin face, dark, sad eyes and a generous mouth. It was the face of a poet or a musician. 'I remember mummy,' Baruch said, finally, speaking slowly in accented English.

'You do?'

'Yes, we make wiz trimmings.' He pointed to a mound of linen in the corner of the room. 'It vas somesing different so I remember.'

'Was it difficult?'

Baruch shrugged: 'Jabber Jukes bought sticks. And we make mummy. Put cloth round and round like this.' With fluent hands, Baruch sketched the shape of a mummy in the air. 'It vas not easy get right shape.'

'What kind of name is Jabber Jukes?' I asked.

As soon as the name was out of my mouth the atmosphere in the tiny room changed. I could feel the tension crackling around me, several of the men paused in their stitching to watch us. Baruch was about to answer my question, then he looked at Sara and stopped.

'Jabber Jukes,' I persisted. 'Who is Jabber Jukes?'

I saw Rachel's gaze, fixing in fright on something behind me. I turned around. A new person was in the room, a spindly little fellow. Hairless as a hard-boiled egg on top, yet with a bushy beard dangling from his chin. He was the sort of being who moves as stealthily as smoke and shadow. I do not know how long he had been in the room, how much of our conversation he had heard. Though the man was as skinny as the other workers, his decent suit marked him out as a man of relative wealth. I knew at once this was Moses Zwingler, Sara's uncle and the owner of the sweatshop.

He muttered something quickly to Sara, then turned on Waldo.

'Permit me to enquire, good sir, what you are doing in my factory while my shop is shut?' Though his voice was silky, there was no mistaking the anger hidden underneath.

We stood there gawping at him. I'm usually quick at thinking of excuses. Not today. My brain had chosen this moment to shut down.

Luckily Baruch, the greener, rescued us:

'De lady wants blouse, Mr Zwingler,' he said, holding up a garment, a shirt of the most revolting mauve.

Instantly I took the way out he had offered: 'I had a fancy for a blouse in this colour, Mr Zwingler. Your niece was kind enough to say she had one in the workshop. I'm afraid I bullied her into bringing me in here to see for myself.'

'We have plenty of blouses in the shop.'

'Not in exactly this shade of mauve.'

'It was not necessary to have come here, my niece would have fetched it,' Mr Zwingler said, but he took the blouse from Baruch. 'I vill let you 'ave it for four shillings. A bargain, young lady, the cloth is of the finest calico.'

Sheer robbery. However, we had little choice if we didn't want to get Mr Zwingler's niece into further trouble. I produced a sovereign from my purse and held it out to Mr Zwingler. The coin lay in my palm, glinting gold. Men stopped working, mesmerised, watching the ordinary coin, as if it were one of the wonders of the world.

'A lady of means,' Zwingler chuckled, delighted. 'Come through. I will fetch your change.'

I reddened as I followed Zwingler, aware that I had been silly to have produced such a large amount of money.

Once we were outside the shop Waldo and Isaac burst into hoots of laughter, while Ahmed looked puzzled. I took the shirt out of the packet Mr Zwingler had wrapped it in and held it up, staring at it in disgust. It was horrible, trimmed with dozens of frills and furbelows, sleeves as puffed as hot-air balloons, a row of fussy bows down the front.

'You'd almost pass for a *girl* in that,' Waldo smirked.

'The *colour*,' Rachel said, with a slight shudder. I had to agree it was an absolutely horrible shade of mauve.

'I don't know, Rachel,' Waldo smirked at my friend. 'Kit would look almost pretty in it. Provided it was at night, of course, and she was at the other end of a dark alley.'

I flashed Waldo a look to let him know how feeble I thought his attempt at wit. 'I will never, ever wear this horrid thing,' I said. 'I know, I'll give it to the Minchin. It is just her sort of thing.' A fit of giggles overtook me at the thought of our governess in the awful blouse.

Rachel made an annoyed noise, sobering us up. 'What are we going to do now? I'm tired, Kit; I want to go to your aunt's house.'

'No.' Waldo shook his head. 'We have detecting to do.'

For once, I agreed with him. 'That's right. We need to find out about this mystery man, Jabber Jukes. Zwingler's men made the mummy but it was Jabber who paid for it.'

'Jabber Jukes,' said Waldo. 'Sounds like a hoodlum.'

'I think,' Ahmed began and stopped. We all looked at him, surprised he'd ventured an opinion without being asked. There was something taller and more confident about him here, in these slums. It was amazing, too, how quickly his English was improving.

'Yes?' Rachel encouraged.

'They were scared,' Ahmed said. 'Very scared.'

'Who was scared?'

'The men – how you say "greeners" – they not like Jabber Jukes.'

'Yes.' Rachel nodded. 'Scared for their lives, I would say. Everyone went all still – like Baruch had done the wrong thing.'

❧ Chapter Nine ❧

'Why is it wrong to call Frenchmen frogs?' my aunt barked at us, as soon as we entered her drawing room, weary and downcast from our trip to Spitalfields.

'Because it is wrong to make rude remarks about people. Especially people you don't know personally,' Rachel ventured, timidly.

'Of course not, you ninny. Rebecca, is it?' Aunt Hilda flashed her a withering look.

'Rachel.'

'That's a particularly wet remark, Rebecca. The answer, of course, is that the comparison is unfair to perfectly decent animals.'

Aunt Hilda was slumped on the sofa, a half-empty glass of whisky in her hand, her face flushed. Something in the newspaper in front of her, the *Pall Mall Gazette*, had clearly angered her. Edging over to see what was wrong I spotted the headline:

FRENCHMAN GASTON CHAMPLON CALLS FAMOUS
LADY EXPLORER, HILDA SALTER, 'A LIAR'.
RELATIONS WITH FRANCE AT RISK.

There was only one thing for it; I would have to distract
her. Once Aunt Hilda was on her favourite subject of
French treachery she would never stop.

'London is terribly smoggy –' I began but Waldo
seized the newspaper and read out the headline.

'You should sue the blighter!' he declared.

'Splendid idea! What a sensible boy,' Aunt Hilda
crowed. 'I'll bet Champlon hasn't the nerve to try his
luck before an honest English jury!'

Quietly I signalled to the others that we should go.
We sidled out as Aunt Hilda declared her intention of
writing a letter to the Queen, protesting 'French
Insolence'. She wouldn't be satisfied, I thought, till
blood had been shed over her stolen mummy.

We were tired and felt oddly listless. We trooped
upstairs and slumped in the piano room, kicking off our
shoes. I, for one, was overwhelmed by our trip to the
sweatshops of the East End. Some of those begging in
the gutters were children, boys and girls even younger
than us. The whole trip left me feeling odd about being
Kit Salter. The daughter of a father who can clothe and
feed me, have me decently educated. (Yes, even the

Minchin counts as a decent education.) How lucky I was to be me. Not one of the unfortunates of the earth doomed to exist among dirt and drudgery.

'We'll have to go back there tomorrow,' I said.

On the faces around me I saw blank looks, which depressed me.

'It's a wild goose chase,' said Isaac.

'Hopeless,' Rachel agreed.

'Waste of time,' Waldo added.

'Well, see if you can think of anything cleverer,' I snapped. 'All you lot can do is moan. Why don't *you* try coming up with a plan?'

A rap on the door interrupted our argument. It was my aunt's maid Mary, carrying a brown envelope. 'Someone knocked at the door, left this for you, miss,' she said.

I turned the envelope over. It was grubby, marked with dirty fingerprints, but was not addressed to anyone.

'How do you know it was for me?'

Mary flushed. 'It was a man wot brung it. A foreign man, all ragged and dirty-like but handsome if you take my meaning. He said it was for the bossy lady. I thought it was your aunt, miss, meaning no offence. But the man, he said no. The bossy *young* lady.'

The others tittered. It was my turn to flush. 'Thank you, Mary,' I said and took the envelope from her.

Casting a cross glance at my friends I slowly opened it and extracted the slip of paper inside. What was written there was enough to make me forget my hurt feelings:

You are not I think a lady to be scared so I will tell you about Jabber Jukes. I will come to big duke hyde in park. 1 O' Clock. Do not be late.

❧ Chapter Ten ❧

'He's not going to come,' I said, despairingly.

We had been waiting under the statue of the Duke of Wellington in Hyde Park for over half an hour. It was a splendid spot, a place to show Ahmed how glittering London could be. All around us nature was in full bloom, over there the fashionable world trooping their thoroughbred horses down Rotten Row. You could admire the broughams of countesses with their golden crests, the carriages of earls. If, like Waldo, your tastes ran to ogling young ladies, you could watch the daintiest in the land, riding side-saddle, dresses flowing elegantly over their horses' flanks.

However, I had not come here for sightseeing. I was bored and cross as I saw my plans unravel once more.

'Patience,' Isaac said, not looking up from the screws he was fiddling with.

None of the others seemed as bothered as I was. Rachel was pointing the sights out to Ahmed, Waldo lounged on the grass, whistling.

'What are you doing, anyway?' I asked Isaac.

'Portable RollerShoes,' he said, holding up two small wheels. 'I've put the brackets for them on my own boots. I'm just working it so I can snap them on and off.'

My mind wandered off as Isaac talked. I had spotted a hunch-backed figure walking past the fence. Was it, could it be? As the figure moved nearer my heart leapt. Yes! It was Baruch the greener, weighed down by something on his back. We ran towards him and said our hellos over the fence.

He made no apologies for his lateness. 'Come with me,' he motioned to us. 'I am hurry. We will have to walk.'

Obediently we left the park and followed him. He set quite a pace, even carrying his large bag of clothes. I had to trot to keep up with him. As Baruch walked, he talked.

'I am taking risk because I like you.' He nodded at me. 'I think you brave.'

'Thank you,' I muttered. I noticed, with a burst of secret satisfaction, that Waldo looked annoyed.

'Also I have 'nother reason.' He halted abruptly.

'Yes?' I prompted and then wished I hadn't spoken for Baruch looked at me so furiously, I shrank back.

'I am angry,' he said. 'So angry it hurts.' He gestured

to his heart. 'You will have to be clever with what I tell you. Not just brave. This is important because these are bad men. Many people, good people are trusting you. You unnerstan' me?'

'Yes.' I nodded, though I wasn't sure what he was talking about.

'Good. Jabber Jukes is a bad man. But he is a small bad man. A young man learning all the hard ways. You unnerstan'?'

'He is an apprentice,' Rachel said. 'An apprentice in evil.'

'Yes. Jabber is young, maybe thirteen or fourteen years old. He works for criminals and they teach him how to be bad.'

'How do you know him?' I asked.

The pavements along Park Lane were crowded with gentry in their fine clothes, but also with working people going about in the noise and bustle that is everywhere in London. I had to raise my voice to get Baruch to hear me. The greener, with his large bundle, struggled to make a path through the crowds.

'What can I say? My master should tell the police about these villains,' Baruch said, stopping in the middle of the pavement. 'But he does not. He is too scared.'

'Moses Zwingler?' I asked, surprised. He didn't look like a particularly nervous man.

'Yes, we are scared. Zwingler, the other shopkeepers, workers, all of us in Raven Row. Every week Jabber or another man – they come and take money. Sometimes they demand five shillings. Sometimes ten. Once they took a whole guinea. And the masters, they pay. The criminals, they say they need the money to protect us.' Baruch shrugged. 'All lies. If the shopkeepers don't pay, they get beaten. Or their shop will be fired.'

'That's wicked.'

'It is the way. Jews, we have many peoples bleeding us. Like lemons – even if we have not much juice there is a little more they can squeeze.'

'I thought it was your master, Moses Zwingler, doing the squeezing,' I said.

Baruch grimaced: 'Fleas feed on small fleas. Both are sucked dry by bigger, how you say?'

'Insects?' I suggested. 'Businessmen?'

'They call it business,' he agreed. 'In Russia it is the same.'

'Who is doing this to you?' Isaac asked. 'Who are these criminals?'

'Where do we find them?' I added.

But Baruch frowned; this talk was making him angry. He turned round and began walking much more quickly. We were on the edge of a crowd, waiting on the pavement. As we approached a large red omnibus appeared from the direction of Victoria. It was emblazoned with signs for Fry's Cocoa and was already packed: gentlemen spilling off the rails at the top, ladies crammed into the downstairs compartment.

People surged around us. We were trapped in a stampede, people pushing and shoving like navvies. An elderly lady in a lace-trimmed bonnet landed me a punch in the ribs as she made her way determinedly past. Baruch was caught in the middle.

'Baruch,' I yelled. 'Where do we find these thugs?'

'You've got to go to Norfolk. To Punch, its a –' abruptly his words were bitten off. I caught a surprised look on his face and then he was lost from view in the human traffic.

'Baruch, Baruch,' I yelled. The others added their voices to mine. It was no good, a second omnibus had driven up and the crowd frothed around it like an angry sea. We would just have to wait till the crush eased.

I glared at a gentleman in a shiny new top hat who had trodden on my foot. If he could afford a hat like that he could also afford manners, was the way I saw it. Another man, with piggy eyes and no chin, shoved against me and, fed up now, I shoved back. We waited for the crowd to disperse and in a few moments most of them had managed to cram into the two omnibuses.

But Baruch was nowhere to be seen. Had he left us? It

made no sense, he was just about to tell us the name of the villain.

Over the rumble of horses' hooves and carriage wheels I suddenly heard screaming. It was Rachel. I looked over at her, frowning. This wasn't the moment for one of her attacks of nerves. My friend was shrieking hysterically, her whole body trembling. I looked down, following her eyes. Baruch was spread-eagled in the gutter – one arm still cradling his sack. There was a trickle of dark liquid coming out of his mouth. He has a dirty face, I thought, for a moment before I realised what the stuff was. Something was sticking out of his shirt-front. Something white and lustrous. I bent down to take a closer look at it and it was all I could do to stop myself screaming. It was the hilt of a pearl-handled knife.

Chapter Eleven

I caught the merest glimpse of Baruch before Waldo jumped in front of Rachel and me, shielding us from the body.

'This is no time to act like my grandfather,' I snapped.

'A corpse isn't a fit sight for young ladies.'

'I'll make up my own mind, thank you very much.' I tried to shoulder my way past him. 'Let go! I need to help Baruch!'

It's true I have never seen a human corpse, but I've seen the bodies of plenty of rabbits and pheasants which have been mauled by foxes. Why is it that us girls are considered such silly creatures that we have to be protected from anything upsetting?

No one offered to help, no one ran to fetch a doctor. Costermongers, top-hatted clerks, flower-girls, everyone circled round the corpse, gawping like fools. There wasn't one person in among them who was willing to take charge. Never had I felt so lost in this giant city. It was just the five of us; mere helpless children and the body with the knife sticking out of its chest.

Reluctantly, Waldo moved aside. My breakfast lurched inside me. The body of a man is quite different from that of a rabbit. Baruch's eyes were open, but quite blank. His skin had a sheeny look, like one of Madame Tussaud's waxwork dummies. That awful blood kept running from his mouth.

I took off my cape and knelt down by Baruch with some idea of placing it under his head. I knew it would not make him more comfortable in death , but it seemed more respectful. But something, some small movement made me jerk back in surprise.

'He's still alive.'

'I think you're right, Kit,' Waldo picked up Baruch's wrist. I noticed there was blood congealing on the greener's index finger, smeared along the palm. He must have tried to grab the knife. 'There's a pulse.'

'Do you think we should take out the knife?' Rachel asked, pointing to the mother-of-pearl hilt sticking out from Baruch's shirt, but I shook my head.

'No. We could rupture an artery or something. Quick, we need to get him to hospital.'

'Help! Stop! Cabby!' Isaac was already halfway in the street, trailing Ahmed behind him.

I turned and a pair of black trousers loomed above

me. Looking up, I saw a young man wearing a uniform with blue jacket and a domed hat. A London policeman!

'Thank heavens you've arrived. He's still alive.'

''Ow did this happen, miss?' the bobby asked.

'We were talking to him and then he went into the crowd and he was knifed. You see it, there –'

'Was 'e robbed?' The policeman asked, finally blowing his whistle for a cab.

'I don't think so. Actually I don't know. Baruch is a greener. He was trying to tell us something important and –'

'A greener, you say?'

'Yes, why?'

'Thought he was your groom. Young lady like you should have a groom or a footman with you when you're out and about.' The policeman knelt down to take a closer look at the body. 'Fellow needs a good wash.'

'He needs more than a wash,' I said hotly. 'He needs a doctor.'

At last a hansom carriage responded to the constable's whistle. The driver, a stout man in a loud check jacket, got out of his cab in a leisurely fashion and joined us on the pavement. Why were they all so slow?

'Greener been attacked. Gonna have to get him to hospital,' the policeman explained.

'As you say, guv'nor.'

'Problem is don't know who's gonna pay. These greeners don't have two brass farthings to rub together.'

Here was a man's life at stake and all they could do was stand around chatting.

'I'll pay,' I said delving into my pocket to pull out my money. My hand curled around empty space. My purse had gone. It was humiliating, awful. I had survived the East End unscathed only for this to happen in the most fashionable park in London. Luckily my purse only contained a couple of shillings, I'd left my remaining two guineas at home. 'I've been robbed,' I blurted.

Everything seemed to slow down. 'Robbery's a very grave matter,' the policeman said, pulling out his notebook. 'Greener did it, you think?'

'NO, I DO NOT THINK!' I snapped, in total exasperation. 'FORGET ABOUT THE ROBBERY. PLEASE, JUST GET THIS MAN TO HOSPITAL.'

Rachel, who was kneeling by Baruch, looked the police constable in the eye. Her face was very grave under her halo of dark curls. 'You don't want this man's death on your conscience,' she said softly. 'He is a good fellow.'

Something in her tone seemed to finally pierce the bobby's thick hide. He shuffled awkwardly, while Waldo pulled out his wallet: 'Here's three shillings,' Waldo said.

'Should be enough to get Baruch to the hospital and pay for a doctor.'

The sight of the money spurred the bobby and the cabby into action. The cabby lifted Baruch under the shoulders and the policeman took his feet. The body looked limp, lifeless. But as they picked him up Baruch's feet thrashed about. He groaned, a sound that was both heart-rending and hopeful. In a matter of seconds he was loaded into the carriage. I wanted to go with him, but there was only room for one more and everyone insisted it should be Waldo.

'I'll make sure he's looked after!' Waldo shouted out of the hansom as it clipped away down Park Lane at a terrific pace.

As I know from numerous schoolroom spats, Waldo is nothing if not stubborn. I was confident that Baruch was in safe hands and prayed that he would recover.

'Now, miss, let's have everything you can recall about the robbery,' the policeman had got his inevitable notebook back out.

'You're not interested in the attack on the greener? Baruch is lying at death's door!'

'Er, might as well give us some stuff on the attack while you're at it.'

We did as he asked. I couldn't help feeling, though, that this policeman's shiny uniform was more impressive than his detecting skills. In fact, if he caught either Baruch's attacker or the thief who had stolen my purse I would eat his hat – felt, board, metal badge and all! The policeman kept us talking for what seemed like a never-ending time, as we trawled through the events of our day: why we were meeting Baruch, what we were doing in the East End and on and on. I had to think up some stories pretty fast. He even seemed disposed to question Ahmed and find out who he was, which frightened our Egyptian stowaway unnecessarily. In the end, when his questions were skirting a little too near the truth, I only managed to get rid of him by saying that my aunt 'the countess' was expecting us to lunch. At the mention of gentry he turned bright red and put away his notebook.

After he had finally left I turned to the others. 'Isaac, you'll have to go to the shop. Tell Moses Zwingler, Baruch has been attacked.'

Rachel hesitated. 'That might not be the best thing for Baruch,' she said.

'What do you mean?'

'Well, how is Moses going to react when he finds out Baruch was talking to us?'

She was right.

'Well, you better go with Isaac then, Rachel. See if you can get to the niece, what's her name again?'

'Sara.'

'See if you can get Sara alone. Tell her what's happened. She can make out she heard about the attack on Baruch in some other way. I'll take Ahmed and I'll go to the Norfolk place Baruch mentioned.'

'What on earth are you saying, Kit? You can't tramp all over Norfolk looking for a Punch and Judy show. It will take you several days to get there for a start and –'

'You've got it wrong,' I said. 'Think about it! East End villains don't go travelling about in the remote countryside. Baruch didn't mean Norfolk the county. The Norfolk Punch's a gin palace in Drury Lane. I saw it from the omnibus this morning.'

Rachel and Isaac could have been twins. The very same obstinate, disapproving look crossed both their faces.

'A tavern!' Isaac said.

'You can't go into a *low* gin palace. By yourself, of all things,' Rachel added.

'She not alone,' Ahmed said. 'I go with Kit.'

'You heard,' I said. 'Ahmed's coming with me.'

'Kit!' brother and sister protested.

I held up my hand to quiet them down. I can also be fairly stubborn when I want to. 'Don't try and stop me. Not if you're my friends. I dragged Baruch into this. I *owe* it to him to stop these criminals – whoever they are.'

❧ Chapter Twelve ❧

Steamy, gin-scented fumes gusted out of the Norfolk Punch, as I opened the door. For a moment I staggered. There was so much alcohol in the air I felt woozy just breathing it in. Mid-morning and the place was already crowded with customers: men, women and even children. Some of them were covered in greasepaint. Actors, perhaps, from the theatres nearby. They were perched on stools by the bar, endlessly reflected in glorious mirrors and sheets of crystal which in the brilliance of gaslight gave the whole interior a fantastic, fairytale feel.

'This is . . .' Ahmed began and faltered as words failed him.

It was indeed. Grander than any other tavern I had glimpsed; a cathedral, almost, of gin. The boards blaring forth from the walls in gold and red could be the signs of some new religion:

OLD TOM CREAM OF THE HEAVENS UNIQUE BALMORAL MIXTURE, AS DRUNK BY HIS HIGHNESS, PRINCE ALBERT

'Women and even children . . . babies . . . drinking alcohol. In Egypt we believe alcohol is . . . how do you say? . . . too bad, evil.' Ahmed looked thoroughly shocked, gazing around at the customers who packed the tavern.

'It certainly isn't a good idea to drink gin in the morning.' I entered, pushing my way past a clump of cab drivers. 'I should expect it finishes you off for the rest of the day.' I noticed Ahmed was not following me, but had halted at the door as if scared to enter.

'Come on,' I said, gently tugging at his sleeve. 'Don't be afraid. We'll go to the bar. I've heard the pot-boys in these places are a wonderful source of gossip.'

We passed a pot-boy in a grubby apron taking several large tankards to customers. I thought it foolish to make enquiries before buying ourselves some drinks with the pennies I had remaining in my pockets – the ones the thief had not managed to steal. As we fought our way to the bar we came up behind a person with carroty hair who was talking in a loud voice. The landlady, busy dispensing glasses of gin, did not seem much interested.

'Nah,' Carrots was saying. 'Them ole tales don't frighten me. People say to me, they say Bob me ole son, you'd be right tickled if you –'

''Old on a mo,' the landlady turned round to serve someone else, then smiling she asked: ''Ow's Velvet? Haven't seen 'er for ages. Too good for us now, is she?'

'Movin' up in the world is ole Nell.' The landlady hadn't waited for his reply, but moved away to serve someone else. However the red-haired boy continued in a loud, bragging voice, not seeming to care if anyone was listening. 'Hardest master in the game is Velvet Nell. She'll not take no lip from no one. Some people fink she's soft just cos she's a gel but they couldn't be more wrong. A monster that's what she is!'

'He spiks different English to you,' Ahmed whispered to me. 'A different sound.'

'It's called a Cockney accent. It comes from East London,' I explained.

'Strange,' Ahmed said, with a grin. 'Maybe I should learn to spik Cockney.'

'Don't you dare,' I hissed. 'Aunt Hilda would never forgive me!'

Meanwhile the youth was still blabbering: 'Yer want sumfink to frighten the little kiddiwinks, don't bother with fairy tales. Them monsters and fings, yer know, made up fings like Spring Heeled Jack, they ain't frightenin'. Yer send them to Nell.'

'I wouldn't wish that on any brat!' the landlady grinned, finally taking some notice of the red-haired boy. 'That'll be ha'pence,' she said to another customer, a grinning old woman wearing a straw hat from which draggled a floppy artificial rose. The old dame weaved away unsteadily, gin slopping down the side of her glass. In fact the pitted pewter counter was awash with gin. Some of the drinkers were so beside themselves they spilt as much of their precious liquid as they drank. I had heard that thrifty landlords collected these leftovers – made up as much of spit as gin – and resold them as 'All-Sorts'.

'Here, wot's this I heard on the grapevine about Velvet branchin' out?' the landlady asked the chattering redhead. 'I 'eard she's moving on, she is, going to get herself into a whole new game.'

'That's wot I bin trying to tell you, if you'd only bin listening. Too good for you, I'll be soon. You won't catch me 'ere no more but down one of them gent's clubs in Pall Mall,' he replied.

'They wouldn't let you in, not till you had a scrub-up and got yourself a new set of threads.' The landlady looked him up and down. 'Nah, I don't fink them toff's club would ever let you in.'

'Less lip.' From behind we saw the youth lean forward

on the bar. 'Give me another glass o' your finest gin, there's a dear.'

'Not yer usual All-Sorts? What's this, Jabber? Nell given you a pay rise now you're leaving Petticoat Lane behind?' The landlady smirked as she filled his glass.

I froze. Two things had galvanised me. The mention of Petticoat Lane and if I'd heard right the landlady called this youth, whose face I couldn't see, Jabber. Jabber Jukes, the criminal apprentice we sought! If so, I understood how he had earned his nickname. He was jabbering on, prattling away non-stop. Judging by his back view, the boy looked rather stringy and insignificant. Shorter than either Ahmed or me.

I tapped the red-haired youth on the shoulder and he turned round, all indignant.

''Ere, wot do you think –' he began.

'Are you Jabber Jukes?'

'Eh?' the boy scowled. His skin was as carroty as his hair. A snub nose, a blaze of freckles, beady, darting eyes. He was wearing an oversize man's coat that swamped his tiny body and the uniform of a swaggering criminal: peaked cap, white neckerchief, red waistcoat and huge trousers fastened with a fancy metal studded belt. He was dressed tough, certainly, but was this little rascal really the person who had so frightened the greeners?

'Jabber Jukes?' Ahmed repeated.

"Oo's your posh friends, Jabber?' the landlady asked, smirking.

So we were on the right track, 'Jabber' was too much of an unusual name for it to be a coincidence. I moved towards him, intent on questioning him, while he regarded us with a cocky smile.

'Do yer want a drop o' gin?' he leered at me. "Ave one on the handsomest boy in the Norfolk Punch. It'd only be right to treat a pretty lady like you.' Poking a dirty thumb at Ahmed he added. 'Yer pal will 'ave to pay for hisself.'

I ignored the less-than-generous offer and looked him straight in the eye: 'I've heard all about you, Jabber Jukes. Does the name Moses Zwingler mean anything to you?'

He met my eye with an insolent smirk.

'Perhaps you'll remember a mummy made of twigs?' I continued.

My words hit their target. Immediately a change came over the boy, his cocksure air dropping away. He jumped off his stool, as the landlady looked on, clattering into me and making me stagger backwards. With one hand he seized my arm and tried to pull me through the pub. In his left hand Jabber was carrying a package, about the size of a family Bible – though I doubt its contents were in any way holy.

'Get off!' I yelled, while Ahmed tried to push him away. It wasn't easy. Jabber was far stronger than he looked.

'Shush!' the strange boy begged. 'Please shut yer mouf, ladyship.'

'I certainly will not.'

'Please, not 'ere.'

Jabber looked so frightened all of a sudden, I relented. He dragged me to a dark corner that was shaded from the gaslight that made the rest of the gin palace so dazzling. Ahmed followed, glaring at Jabber angrily.

'Yer gotta go. Right now. I know who yer are. If I'm seen with yer I'm dead,' Jabber explained as he tried to push me down on a wooden bench that stood behind a table, in a shadowy corner of the room.

Theories flashed through my mind as he talked. He knew who I was. How? Had the gang heard about our enquiries at Zwinglers? Had they followed Baruch and seen us with the greener? Were the gang on the lookout for us? If so they must have a fearsome organisation. After all, it was only yesterday that the five of us had visited Moses Zwingler's shop. There were so many possibilities. It was as if I was blindfolded and playing a game of badminton against a far superior opponent. I had to admit it to myself, for the first time I felt out of my depth.

'I'm not going anywhere,' I said. 'Not till you answer my questions, Jabber Jukes.'

''Ow do yer know that?' he yowled, he was towering over me as I sat on the bench. 'Me moniker is sumfink between me and me maker.'

'Pardon?' I asked. This boy's speech was so foreign to me he could have come from the wilds of Africa rather than the capital city of my own country.

''Ow do yer know me?' Jabber said. He sat down on one of the stools opposite me, besides Ahmed.

'He wants to know how you know his name,' Ahmed intervened. Brilliant! An Egyptian understood this hooligan better than I did!

'I have my sources.'

'Bet yer just makin' it up.'

'I'll come down to Petticoat Lane looking for you,' I said with a burst of inspiration. 'I'll say you're my friend. I'll tell everyone you were jabbering on. That you couldn't stop telling me your secrets. I'll tell them I saw you talking to the police.'

'I ain't no blower,' he protested indignantly.

'Pardon?' He'd lost me again. Blower? What could he mean?

'I ain't about to nose to the rozzers.'

Finally! Something I could understand.

'I'm not asking you to speak to the police. I just want

102

you to answer my questions.'

''Ow did yer find me, anyhow?' All the time we were talking Jabber's eyes were darting around the gin palace, as if to check that no one was watching us. I resolved to capitalise on his unease, by hitting him with all I knew.

'I have my ways. Understand? Now listen, Jabber, I know that you are part of a filthy, rotten criminal gang. I'm sure the police will be very keen to hear all about it. I know you take protection money from the shopkeepers of Raven Row –'

'That ain't for me –' he interrupted. 'That's for the captain.'

'What captain? Who are you talking about?'

'It's wot you 'ave in the navy,' he replied, with a smirk, as if I had somehow shown myself up.

'Who's "the captain", Jabber? I'll warrant your "captain" has never been to sea. Remember I can make things very hot for you.'

''Is name is Napoleon Bonaparte.'

'Don't you play the fool with me.'

I had lost my advantage somehow, in some way that I didn't understand. Jabber seemed to relax a bit, he leant forward, a honeyed smile spreading over his face: 'You're pretty, miss, close up.'

I flushed, and then, cross with myself, scowled.

'A right beauty you are, miss.' He arranged his brown

teeth in what he probably thought was a charming smile. 'Though if you don't mind my saying so you could do with a dash of powder.'

There was a caricature of a disgusting old man in Jabber's manner as he simpered at me. He must believe he was being smart and manly. It was all I could do not to laugh in his face. No one has ever called me 'pretty' or begged me to wear powder. Not even my dear papa, who would love me to be a little more ladylike.

I was just contemplating giving Jabber a smack across the face for his presumption when suddenly a whistle screeched. With amazing speed the gin palace filled up with blue uniforms. Conical helmets towered above the top hats, bonnets and bowlers. Stout boots tramped upon the floor. It was a sight to instil fear into the hearts of wrongdoers, who miraculously melted away. If Ahmed had not grabbed Jabber by his arm, our young friend would have vanished too.

'The bluebottles,' he yelped, struggling to get out of Ahmed's grasp.

'I know.' I nodded. I was getting the hang of Jabber's way of talking. 'The rozzers are here.'

'Let me go, gerroff me.' Jabber had wriggled out of his coat but Ahmed had grabbed him by the arm. 'It's a raid, you ignorant heathen.'

There was a policeman a few feet from our table. A

tall young man, carrying a stout truncheon and a pair of handcuffs. A grin adorned his rosy face, which became larger as he saw our scoundrel friend. He just had to pass through two men, actors covered in greasepaint, and he would be upon us.

'I'm for the block house,' Jabber moaned, seeing the policemen advance and realising that this time there was no way out. 'Yer gotta help me.'

He collapsed on the table, his head in a pool of beer. Meanwhile under the table something banged into my skirt. My hands knew what it was before my brain did. It was the package wrapped in cloth which Jabber had been carrying. Calmly I took it, though my heart was beating fast. My hands trembling slightly, I placed it in my bag, careful to show nothing on my face.

'Gin? At this time o' the morning!' the policeman towered over our table. 'Watch out, Jabber, or you'll end up in the workhouse like your ole ma.'

'Jus' a drop o' ale to wet me tonsils.'

'Come on, lad, I'm taking you in.' Sullenly Jabber stood up and the policeman clapped a pair of handcuffs on him. Then he noticed me. 'This rascal not been bothering you, miss, has he?'

'Not at all,' I said, calmly. 'I've had a hard morning shopping and was feeling rather faint so I came in here to sit down. Rather a strange place.' I looked around the gin palace with an innocent air.

My act had worked. 'You shouldn't come in here, miss,' the policeman said, in a fatherly tone. 'I can see you're a respectable young lady. This is no place for you. The Norfolk Punch attracts a bad lot. In fact, miss, we've had a tip-off about this 'ere gin palace. It's a den of thieves.'

'Thank you. I am just leaving.' I rose, Ahmed following suit.

'Hang on.' The policeman looked Ahmed over, taking in his foreign looks. 'Who's this?'

'My friend and guest, officer.'

'How long you known 'im?' The policeman was scanning Ahmed up and down, taking in his good clothes. Perhaps they were too good? 'See, the thing is we been warned about bad elements in the Punch,' the policeman continued.

'Ahmed's not a bad element.'

'He's a foreigner.'

'So?'

'You can never be too sure wiv foreigners.'

The policeman hadn't taken his eyes off Ahmed while the whole exchange was going on, a scrutiny I could see was making the Egyptian boy very nervous. Suddenly Ahmed bolted, leaving my side and trying to dash past the policeman to the door. The fool! He had no hope of making it, the Punch was far too crowded. The policeman put out a hand and caught him by his coat-tails, causing Ahmed to crash to the floor. Bending down, the policeman produced a second pair of handcuffs and in a moment Ahmed was stoutly cuffed as well. That scoundrel Jabber was smirking as he watched the scene.

'How dare you!' I raged to the policeman.

'If he's not a bad 'un why'd he try to scarper?' the policeman asked.

'You frightened him,' I snapped. Poor Ahmed did look terrified, his wrists shackled to a chain which the policeman carried. His doe eyes flitted around wildly, searching for a way out, but finding none. They came back to me and I couldn't resist the pleading in them.

'Let him go at once,' I said, in my most commanding voice. 'Ahmed El Kassul, is my friend and guest. My aunt, the countess, shall hear about this! And my father, the Bishop!'

A slight shadow passed over the policeman's face but he stood his ground. 'Sorry, young lady, I got no choice. I'll have to take him in,' he said.

I was so angry it was all I could do to control my temper. At the same time, Ahmed's obvious desperation, made me feel terribly guilty. I glared at the policeman but at the same time my heart was beating a scared rhythm. I had landed us in a horrible mess. I'd taken a package from

Jabber with absolutely no idea what was inside. If the policeman searched my bag, and found something criminal, I would go to prison too! How then would I free Ahmed? What would my father and Aunt Hilda say?

'We're taking 'em all to Covent Garden Police Station,' the policeman said, nodding at me, as if to say that was enough talking. He motioned Ahmed to join Jabber, who, let us be thankful for small mercies, was at least not talking for once. The two of them were marched away, joining the miserable procession of jail-bound men and women. Their shuffling progress from all over the gin palace was endlessly reflected in the huge mirrors. While this was going on, most of the patrons carried on drinking their gin and chatting; watching the arrests with the sort of mild interest that most people show at a schoolboy cricket match.

I staggered against the wall, Ahmed's face swimming before me. A scream came out of me, before I could stop it. Ahmed looked back at me helplessly and a few other patrons turned their eye on me, before resuming puffing on their cigarettes. There was no one here to help me, no one who cared. Before they were led out of the Norfolk Punch Jabber turned his head round and looked straight at me. I was amazed to see he was grinning. His left eye closed in a wink, before the policeman gave him a shove and he vanished out of the door.

◑ Chapter Thirteen ◐

'So, you've had Ahmed arrested and you're carrying a package which probably contains stolen goods. How do you plan to dig yourself out of this hole?' Rachel asked.

'I don't know.' I hung my head, shame boiling inside me.

'You don't know!'

'The police have taken them to Covent Garden station. I'll come up with a plan in a moment.'

'Please! Spare us.' Rachel strode around my aunt's parlour, her skirts swishing in agitation. 'Promise me one thing, Kit, no more plans.'

Nothing Rachel could say would make me feel any worse than I already did. My friends had warned me not to go to the gin palace. But I hadn't listened and now all I had achieved was getting Ahmed arrested. Maybe Rachel was right. Maybe I did need to think more before I acted. While Rachel had cleverly managed to get a message about the attack on Baruch to the tailor's niece

I had achieved . . .

'That's right, Kit. You've achieved nothing. Actually no, that's not true. You have managed something, you've made things much worse,' Rachel said, breaking in on my thoughts.

'Don't go on so,' I begged, casting a glance at the linen-wrapped package which sat on the card table. 'Let's open the package. Maybe it'll help in some way. Give us some clue.'

'Sometimes I think you shouldn't be let out,' Rachel continued relentlessly. 'Not without a dog collar and some groom or chaperone to stand guard over you.'

'I could go to the police station –' I began.

'Certainly not,' Rachel said. 'We'll wait till your aunt gets home. You'll have to explain it to her, somehow, and get her to help you –'

I interrupted. 'I know I'm awful. Will you stop now, please.' Listlessly I picked up the package. String was tied around the coarse, greyish linen. It was about the size of a book, squishy to the touch. I squeezed it: there was something harder inside.

'You don't know what it is. Could be poison. Or a gun,' Rachel said.

'Wrong shape.' I tried biting the string. 'Maybe I can open it with my teeth.'

Silently Rachel held out a pair of embroidery scissors.

Feeling foolish, again, I snipped the string and revealed –
not a pistol, exotic jewels, diamonds. Certainly not
something that would give us a clue to the mummy's
whereabouts. Instead nestling in the wrinkled folds of
cloth was a dirty old dish.

'Just a butter dish!' Rachel blurted.

I looked at the thing that lay in the cloth with mount-
ing excitement. It shone dully under a coating of dirt.

'It's not a butter dish,' I said.

'Certainly it is.' Rachel picked it up, looking closely at
the thing. It was engraved with an odd sort of crest, a
cow like animal. 'An ugly one, at that.' She turned it over
in her palm, puzzled.

'NO!' I shook my head. 'I mean it's not *just* a butter
dish.'

Rachel looked at me, as if I was talking sheer gibber-
ish.

'How did it get into Jabber's hands, I wonder?' I continued, turning my attention back to the dirty cloth
package. I felt in the package, nothing, except a tiny stub
of paper. I took the paper and read the scrawl of writing.

jacko no dirt i want half the
dosh cos i brung the goods. J.

I handed the note to Rachel and strolled over to the

window, my mind working furiously. Should I give Rachel the slip and go to Covent Garden Police Station? I could try and find out which prison Ahmed and Jabber had been taken to, if indeed they had been jailed. Or would they be held in the police station? Would a little bribery work? I'd heard that sometimes one could pay to have minor prisoners released from jail. Meanwhile I had a feeling about the note and the butter dish, I *knew* how we could make it work to our advantage.

It was time I had a good talk with Jabber.

'What in heaven's name does it mean?' Rachel asked, coming over to the window to return the note to me.

'Isn't it obvious?' I couldn't resist the opportunity to get back at Rachel a little, after all she had been lecturing me non-stop.

'No, it isn't.' Rachel replied shortly.

I was about to explain the significance of the butter dish and the note when down in the street I suddenly saw something that made my words dry up. Emerging from the shadows of a hansom cab was a stick of a boy. Something in his outrageous swagger was familiar. Even from the fifth floor there was no mistaking that burst of fiery hair. Jabber Jukes!

Not bothering to explain to Rachel I dashed out of the room and ran pell-mell down the stairs. Jabber was trying to convince Mary to let him in when I got to the front door. From behind him stepped the slight figure of Ahmed.

'Ahmed!' gasped Rachel, who had run after me. 'How glad we are to see you!'

'Jabber,' Ahmed explained shyly, clearly thrilled with his reception from Rachel. 'He freed me.'

'Called in a few favours, I did,' Jabber shrugged. 'Plenty o' folk owe me one.'

While Rachel fussed over Ahmed, I pulled Jabber into the dining room. He gawped at the sideboard laden with crystal, china and silver, the chandelier hanging over the polished table. Maybe estimating how much my aunt's possessions would fetch from one of his criminal friends.

'I don't want you to get any clever notions, Jabber,' I said firmly, with a sudden vision of returning to the house to find it robbed of all valuables. 'I don't want any of your rascally friends after my aunt's silver.'

'Yer got the wrong idea,' he replied, trying to look hurt.

'So, Jabber?'

'I came to say fank you, didn't I? It was right kind of you to save me from the rozzers like that. I'd have got jugged for sure if they found that package on me.'

'What do you mean – jugged?' I asked, my mind wandering back to the note. I would have to play this hardened young criminal carefully. 'You're not a hare.'

Jugged hare was one of Cook's specialities.

'Put inside.' He explained as if I was very stupid. 'Arrested by 'Er Majesty's rozzers and put in prison.'

'Probably the best place for you.' I grinned.

'Oh that's very nice, that is.'

'Only joking. It seems we have to thank you too, for helping Ahmed.'

'One good turn deserves another. Now, can I 'ave me package back?' he gestured at the bundle, which I had in my hand.

I gaped, astounded by his cheek. 'I know what's in the package. I know where you got it from and I know what you planned to do with it!'

'Yer bluffing,' the boy said, regarding me uneasily.

'Oh no, I am most certainly not. I'll warrant, Jabber, that you're pretty quick to seize *any* opportunity. You are a downright thief.'

'Who says?' he stared at me, defiantly.

'I do,' I replied. 'Last night there was a robbery at Lady Mary Leland's house in Belgravia. The thieves stole a quantity of items from the kitchens before they were discovered by the butler and chased out of the house. In the process they shot the dog. It was a cocker spaniel. Totally harmless, I believe.' I threw a newspaper at him, folded on the page with the report of the robbery; it fell on the rug between us. 'The details are all in there.'

'Shame about the mutt,' Jabber murmured looking at the rug. He spoke so low I almost wasn't sure I had heard right.

Slowly I drew the butter dish out of the linen package.

Jabber looked up at me, unapologetic. 'Go on then, Princess, go to the police,' he said, his brown teeth revealed in a wide smirk. 'Course you won't find me, not for dust.'

'That's not what I had in mind.' I smiled.

'Wot?'

'I've something more interesting planned.' I drew the note to 'Jacko' out of the linen package and read it out slowly to Jabber, who didn't flinch. When I had finished there was a moment's silence. 'You must take me for a fool,' I said eventually.

He shrugged, as if to agree with my statement.

'Think again,' I said calmly. 'This isn't just any old dish, it is a very valuable object made of the finest silver. You see, I know *exactly* what that note means. What happened to honour among thieves?'

'Come again?'

'Here's how it happened, Jabber. You didn't just steal that butter dish from Lady Mary Leland. You stole it from your "captain" – what was the name you were blabbering in the Norfolk Punch? "Velvet Nell"? That's it, Velvet Nell. You were planning to send the dish to a receiver of stolen goods, have it melted down for silver and split the proceeds. You were betraying your Velvet Nell – going behind her back.'

'Business is business.'

'Business, is that your name for thieving?' I regarded him steadily. 'I wonder what Velvet Nell will have to say about it?'

He didn't reply; the stream of blabber had finally dried up. There was something cringing about him now – underneath the fancy oversize jacket and the studded belt, Jabber was just a scared boy.

'I don't care about your gang's thieving, I don't care about the protection business. Not at present, anyway. I'm going to help you, Jabber, by keeping quiet about your little swindle. So, I want you to help me in turn.'

'All right, miss.' He was visibly trying to pull himself together again.

'What I want to know about is the fake mummy. Who had it made at Moses Zwingler's workshop? Who is paying?'

A wary look came over Jabber's face and he blinked once or twice. After a moment of this he looked me in the face. 'I'll tell yer, miss, though Velvet Nell, my captain, she'd kill me – you saw what she done to the greener. If she ever finds out about this I'll be pushing up the daisies.'

'Who is this Velvet Nell?'

''Aven't yer 'eard of Velvet Nell? She's right 'ard, is Nell. One of the most feared captains in the whole game. She done the job stealin' that Egyptian mummy and makin' the other at the sweatshop. And the greener –' he paused.

I interrupted: 'She had poor Baruch stabbed, because your gang followed him and saw him talking to us. She must be a monster.' Then another thought occurred to me. 'Were you there at the omnibus stop?'

I saw by his reaction that he was.

'Oh Jabber, you didn't stab Baruch!'

'No, miss, I'm not the killing type. Not by a long straw.'

'Honest?'

'On me own life, miss.'

I was forced to believe him. Jabber didn't strike me as a vicious person. Besides if he was a murderer he wouldn't be here now, would he? Like as not, I would have my throat slit, instead.

'Where is the real mummy?'

Jabber hesitated, thinking up a story no doubt.

'Remember, Jabber, if you lie to me or try and put me on the wrong track, I'll go straight to Velvet Nell with this.' I held up the note.

Jabber groaned. 'Yer know the Alhambra?'

I nodded. It was impossible to miss the famous theatre, towering over Leicester Square, with its massive dome and soaring minarets.

'The Velvet Mob are keeping the mummy there, backstage. In one of them props rooms. We hide things there reg'lar. Our captain, she loves the music hall. You can't miss ole Velvet Nell.'

'Slow down, Jabber. I'm guessing the Velvet Mob is your gang?'

He nodded.

'But why does the Velvet Mob want an ancient Egyptian mummy? Why do they want *this* mummy, so much?'

'Dunno,' Jabber replied frankly. 'Me and Bender we took a good look at the mummy when we were takin' it in the carriage from Oxford to London. We thought –'

'You thought there might be something valuable in it, something you could steal!'

'Not that, miss.' He grinned, but I didn't believe him for a moment. 'Anyways, we took a look and it was only a dried up old fing, wrapped in these smelly bandages. Course we couldn't unwrap the bandages but we had a poke round – blimey how they stank.'

'Natron,' I said absentmindedly. 'The salts used for embalming the mummy. But I still don't understand.

There's a mystery here. What is so special about this mummy to Velvet Nell?'

He shrugged. 'Issa job, innit? I'm only a sergeant. I dunno wot the captain is up to.'

I believed him. But it also made sense that Velvet Nell, a common East End criminal from what I'd deduced, would have no special interest in mummies. She must be stealing it for someone, a person who lurked in the shadows while her gang undertook the dangerous work.

'How can I recognise Velvet Nell?'

'I don't like no skinny ladies. Like me curves as much as any other man.' Jabber grinned. 'Nell is a right ole one, foul temper on her and cruel she can be, but she's a real beauty.' He leered at me. 'Though not as beautiful as you. I tell yer,'

'Enough,' I snapped. 'Tell me about this Nell.'

'Ye can't miss her. Built like an omnibus, she is. And she never wears anything but red velvet.'

'How can I get backstage?'

He shrugged: 'Go as stagehands, so yer won't attract no attention. Jus' slip the ole guy at the stage door a shilling. He won't bovver you.'

'Shush,' I hissed at Jabber. I'd heard footsteps outside. It was only Rachel. She entered the room and stopped short when she saw Jabber. I can read Rachel's mind and I knew she was shocked that he was still here.

'I suppose we have you to thank for getting Ahmed out of jail,' she said to him.

'S'all right, miss.' Jabber turned crimson. He blushed as easily as a debutante. 'Happy to help.'

'I'm grateful to you. Though if it wasn't for Kit, here, Ahmed wouldn't have been arrested in the first place.'

It seemed Rachel still hadn't forgiven me.

'Anyway, Kit, I just came to remind you. Your aunt's back at five.'

I looked at the clock. Ten minutes to five. Aunt Hilda would be here at any moment.

'Jabber's just leaving.'

'Naw I'm not. I'd like a cuppa tea. My throat's parched somefink awful.'

'Jabber, you are leaving. My aunt will be back soon and I don't think she'll be much impressed to find you here.'

Rather grumpily Jabber consented to be shown out. After the shock of finding out I had something against him he had recovered his composure. He sauntered through the place, eyeing the pictures in the hall as if he owned them. As he swaggered down the front steps, I called him back.

'See you at the Alhambra,' I said and my left eye closed in a very Jabber-like wink.

'I'd buy yer a drink. 'Cept it's not good for me health

to be seen wiv yer.'

'I'd pass on the gin, anyway,' I replied and hesitated. I wanted to say something more to him and didn't quite know how to put it: 'Jabber . . .'

'Yeah?'

'I want you to know, I'll keep my side of the bargain. I won't tell your captain anything . . .' I paused, searching for the right phrase. 'I *really* appreciate your help. You've been a gent.'

'That's nicely put, miss,' he said awkwardly.

'Please . . . call me Kit.'

Jabber flushed with pleasure, his mouth opening in a grin that showed all his rotten teeth. He came towards me and for a horrified moment I thought he was going to embrace me. But instead he was pressing my hand. Placing something in it. Something hard and smooth. Surprised I looked down. Three of my aunt's best silver teaspoons glinted in my palm.

'Sorry, Kit,' Jabber muttered, turning his back on me and drawing up the collar of his coat. 'Force of habit.'

❧ Chapter Fourteen ❧

A tightrope stretched across the dome of the Alhambra, way above the fug of cigar smoke, the clink of champagne glasses, the chatter of pretty painted women and their escorts. London's grandest music hall was packed. There were rumours that the Prince of Wales himself was here. He had been an admirer of tonight's star performer, the Great Blondin, since he had seen him walk a rope stretching over the chasm of the Niagara Falls.

Most of the crowd paid no attention to the tattered children who wandered through the great room. Rachel had flatly refused to sneak out in the middle of the night and Ahmed had stayed behind with her. So it was just Waldo, Isaac and me, disguised as stagehands. My stay-at-home friends were missing a treat: the sawdust underfoot, the great crystal chandeliers glimmering above us, the excited diners clustered around their circular tables. Though Waldo claimed to be a regular at the music hall, I had never been anywhere so brash before. *So thrilling!*

As we sneaked about the Alhambra we searched for a huge lady dressed in blazing scarlet. There were plenty of customers who might have passed for Velvet Nell. No one quite striking enough, though. Then I saw a woman, sitting in the midst of a group of men at a circular table, who made me stop dead in my tracks. She was super-colossal, taking up several chairs, oozing pale, soft flesh in every direction. Her fists were like hams, her boots as big as cricket bats. I have strong hands, but they would have looked puny in this woman's palms. To top it all she was swathed in several yards of red velvet, as rich and glossy as blood.

She should have been gross, but she wasn't. She was lovely. Her eyes were sparkling blue, her skin fresh as milk, her lips in the middle of all that flesh like the prettiest pink rosebuds. To top it all, she had thick curls of a particularly vivid shade of red. She glimmered and twinkled, speckled as she was with diamonds and pearls. Even from our position at the promenade at the side of the auditorium I could tell that the tough-looking men around her were half terrified and half in love with her. Velvet Nell sat in the midst of them; a big, beautiful spider, spinning her web. The scoundrels who did her bidding were her flies.

She frightened me. Instinctively, I knew this woman would stop at nothing to get her way. Gathering up my courage, I whispered to the others to wait at the side of the room. Then cautiously I sneaked by Velvet Nell's table. Luckily there was a waiter, serving the next table who hid most of me, though I was but a few inches from the lady's pillowy white shoulders.

'More bubbly,' I heard Velvet Nell drawl, something Irish in the lazy sound of her vowels. 'I've got a thirst on me tonight.'

The man addressed snapped his fingers at the wine waiter, who indicated he would be over as soon as he finished serving his table.

'All set for tonight's lark then?' Nell said, in the same lazy drawl.

The man nodded.

'Make sure you are, sugar,' Velvet Nell said, menace in the very sweetness of her tone. 'This is a big un, this is.'

'I ain't never let you down, Nell,' her thug replied.

'This ain't the time to start, I'm telling you that for free.'

The conversation was just getting interesting but the wine waiter had moved over to Velvet Nell's table to take her order. I couldn't risk being noticed so I slid back to the side of the crowded room, keen to let the others know that the gang planned something – tonight. Waldo, however, had other things on his mind.

'Pssst.' Waldo nudged me, excitedly. 'It's really *him*!'

Sitting at a table laden with oysters and champagne, in the right corner of the room, was a stout, whiskered man. He was surrounded by merry, bejewelled ladies, hearty gents dressed in the height of fashion. I took a second look. If I was not mistaken, Edward, the Prince of Wales, was visiting the Alhambra incognito.

'To think I'm in the presence of royalty,' Waldo gushed. 'Why, I've practically met the future king of England. Mama will be over the moon.'

'Surely your mama is already great friends with the Prince,' I said sarcastically.

'What *are* you talking about?'

'She must have visited Buckingham Palace during one of her seances.' Waldo's mother spent half her money on seances, where a so-called 'medium' would contact the 'spirits' for her. She really was quite foolish on the subject, which I thought was all a sham. Waldo, the adoring son, was far more gullible. I loved to tease him about it.

'Mediums only contact dead people,' he snapped. 'Don't you know anything!'

'Anyway you can't tell her about the Prince,' I said, changing the subject. 'We are here in secret, remember.' Americans love our royal family. I suppose not having one of their own they envy us our gracious Queen and all the pomp and glitter of a court. Though I must admit, Edward Albert in the flesh was certainly no Prince Charming. The Prince of Wales had a reputation for loving the pleasures of the table as much as the company of pretty women I could see, now, how he had got the unflattering nickname 'Tum-Tum'.

I just had time to point out Velvet Nell and her entourage of four men to Isaac and Waldo before there was a great roll of thunder. A beam of limelight flared, illuminating the Great Blondin balancing on the high wire. He was a trim little man, with his hair parted slickly on one side, dressed in tight-fitting short trousers worn over pale stockings. His feet were shod in embroidered satin slippers. They stood daintily on the high wire. He bowed to the crowd, paying special attention to the Prince of Wales. Then, with a flourish, he put on a blindfold and picked up a balancing pole. Blondin was off!

The wire was at least fifty feet above the floor and he had no safety net. If he fell he would surely be smashed to smithereens. I hoped that Blondin was not called 'The Great' for nothing. But we had no time to stand about worrying about the tightrope walker's health. We had to get moving while all eyes were on the show.

Swiftly the three of us made our way to the stage door. There was an old man guarding the exit, probably

to make sure that no drunken or over-enthusiastic gentlemen got through to pester the ballet girls backstage.
As Jabber had told us, he wasn't the type to ask too many
questions. We slipped him a couple of shillings and he
let us through.

Backstage was as hot and crowded as the music hall.
A haze of cigarette smoke lit by the flare of gaslights. A
half-dressed ballet girl ran past me, her pink tutu sticking out over slim legs in pale tights. She was followed by
a flock of others, like flamingos about to descend on a
watering hole. A plaster dolphin was abandoned on the
edge of the wings, its glass eye regarding us fishily.
Everywhere there was a litter of props and prop men,
scene-shifters and muscled acrobats limbering up. And
above it all, the director barking orders. What a strange
combination of backstage chaos and onstage perfection
the music hall was.

Finding the mummy was not going to be easy.
Luckily everyone was so busy with their own concerns
they took no notice of three young stagehands. I was
just about to suggest heading for the stairs leading away
from the wings, when a great gasp went through the
auditorium. Isaac and Waldo poked their heads round
the edge of the curtain. I followed suit. The Great
Blondin had finished his blindfold walk to a storm of
applause. An acrobat brought a wheelbarrow to

Blondin, who was balanced on a ledge at the edge of the Alhambra's great dome. Blondin was proposing to push it along the tightrope! That couldn't be possible, surely? Why, the wheels themselves must be thicker than the wire. With a low bow, gently placing one foot on the tightrope, Blondin addressed a gentleman in the crowd.

'Do you believe I can walk the wire pushing this wheelbarrow?' he asked.

'I think so,' the man answered.

A ripple went through the audience, a flurry of necks craning to see whom the acrobat had picked out. What audacity! He was speaking to the Prince of Wales himself.

'Are you sure?'

'Why not?' the Prince answered.

'Are you absolutely certain?'

'Yes, I'm absolutely certain.'

'Absolutely?

'Absolutely.'

'Then why don't you hop into the wheelbarrow and I'll push you along the tightrope.'

There was utter silence. Waiters, in the midst of pouring glasses of champagne, turned to statues. Gentlemen about to puff on their cigars, stopped stone-dead. The very smoke in the air seemed to freeze. The Prince uttered a genial laugh, and a sigh went through the hall.

He wouldn't take the bet. He couldn't be so reckless. Queen Victoria herself would be outraged.

'Is this a good idea?' the Prince asked.

'I'll guarantee your safety with my life,' Blondin replied.

'You put a lower value on your life than most. But I don't want to spoil your fun. Sir, you're on!'

The Prince rose from the supper table, a smile on his whiskered face. I could see that his friends and attendants were arguing with him, trying to persuade him not to be so foolish. He pushed them off impatiently and walked to the stage. We watched, scarcely believing our eyes, while circus boys helped the portly prince up the ladder to the ledge at the side of the dome. Low murmurings spread through the room. He was prepared to do it. To risk his life and the future of the monarchy for the sake of a silly music-hall stunt!

'Let's go,' I hissed to Isaac and Waldo, who were watching, spellbound. So was every other man, woman and child backstage. 'This is a perfect time. No one will pay any attention to us.'

'You go,' they replied in unison. 'I'm not missing this.'

But I couldn't pull myself away either, as the Prince ascended the steps of a ladder to the top where Blondin was waiting. There was utter silence as he climbed heavily into the wheelbarrow – which I must say looked a very tight squeeze. The front wheel of the barrow was balanced on the tightrope and how it wobbled. Even from way down below I could imagine how queasy the Prince must feel. The Great Blondin made one more bow to the audience. Then he set off, the wheelbarrow with the Prince in front of him. Blondin took a step, and then another. Gosh, it must be impossible to control such a weight on the fragile wire. The wheel of the barrow itself, was bigger, clumsier, than the thin wire. One slip – but it didn't bear thinking about.

On his tenth step Blondin wobbled and a great big *aaaah* went through the crowd. From among the crowd came a single, hysterical shriek, from someone who could no longer bear this. My own nerves were pitched to breaking point. He righted himself swiftly and went on, pushing the wheelbarrow with great skill.

Then, just a few inches from the end of the wire, another wobble. The wheelbarrow steered fractionally wrong, tilted. Blondin's left hand rose in the air. Inside the barrow, the Prince pitched to the right and managed to grab the tightrope. The barrow fell with the speed of a boulder, clanging horribly as it hit the ground. The Prince lost his grip on the rope, he was slipping, slipping . . . Only Blondin could save him now. The tightrope walker was back on the wire, he held out his hand to the lurching prince. It was going to be all right. Blondin closed on the Prince's collar, he reached out strong arms to him. Our royal heir was going to be, *must be*, safe.

Down below the screams stopped, as for an instant, we all gave thanks. Then the collar ripped and appallingly the whole thing spun out of control and the Prince was spiralling downwards through the air. A large dark blob. It was impossible to take it in, it happened so fast. Hysteria overtook the crowd, screams and wails mingling with sobs. Gallant gentlemen rushed forward. An acrobat leapt off the stage to try and catch the Prince, while next to me a ballet girl fainted.

But then something swung out of nowhere, making for the Prince so fast it was a mere blur.

I didn't understand. What was going on?

With a sudden smile the Prince grabbed at the flying object. It was a piece of wood fixed to thick rope. A trapeze! Mid-air, the Prince somersaulted. He tumbled, righted himself. A moment later he had landed firmly on the ground, his chubby body as graceful as a ballet girl.

Incredible! Dumbfounded, the crowd was silent. We watched our acrobat Prince not knowing what to think! Where had he learnt to fly on a trapeze?

One by one, the diners rose, holding their arms aloft, as they clapped and clapped. The ovation of a lifetime for a prince in a million. Modestly, the Prince acknowledged the applause with a smile. As casual as if he took a tumble on the trapeze every day at Buckingham Palace.

Blondin had appeared by Prince's side, like a genie out of a bottle. Not a hair of his brilliantined head was out of place; though triumphant, he was calm. He held up a hand for silence and when the clapping had ceased gave a bow. 'Gentlemen, I give you my assistant Barney,' the Great Blondin shouted, 'and I give special thanks to someone with true sporting blood who has permitted this little imposture. Put your hands together for –' the rest of his words were drowned out as a man, who had been sitting quietly in a shadowy corner of the room, rose. As he stood up his head was illuminated in the flare of a gaslight. Those bushy whiskers, that genial smile. The round cheeks so reminiscent of his mother, Queen Victoria. How could anyone have been taken in by a mere actor? This was the genuine article. Unmistakably the real Prince of Wales! His Royal Highness Albert Edward.

The other man was an acrobat playing the Prince. And the Prince himself was here to witness the trick on his future subjects. What a stunt! Never before had the halls of the Alhambra resounded with such a fever of clapping and cheering.

We couldn't afford to linger, though. 'Look sharp,' I hissed to my friends and dived into the backstage muddle. We wandered past more ballet girls who were getting ready, amongst a froth of pink tutus, for their famous dolphin show. We went down a dark corridor lit by only a couple of spluttering lamps – we had to find the props room.

'Where's Isaac?' I turned around, noticing with a pang of fear that he was not with us. If anything happened to him Rachel would never speak to me again. Hurriedly Waldo and I retraced our steps. Isaac was back in the wings, staring at a small boy who was collecting iron cannon balls and placing them in a wooden box. This was what theatrical folk called the 'thunder run'. It was the boy's job to roll the iron balls down the wooden channel and make the noise we'd heard before Blondin's act – the din of an approaching storm.

'What are you thinking of? Wandering off like this!' I hissed to Isaac.

Isaac came out of his reverie with a start. 'I've had an idea, Kit!'

'Isaac!'

'What?'

'This is not the time for one of your ideas.'

'Thing is . . . I could make a much better system for creating the sound of thunder. If we hung a metal chute from the ceiling, powered it say with a compressed steam engine – the engine could fire off the balls at a rate –'

I grabbed Isaac by the arm and forcibly pulled him

along with me. We turned left, snaking along the same badly lit corridor.

'Isaac,' I blurted with sudden inspiration. 'I've a special job for you.'

'You have?'

'We need a look-out. It's vital – but not in the Alhambra. When we find the mummy we need someone to keep the coast clear.'

'I don't understand.'

'I want you to wait on Charing Cross Road, check for the villains we saw around Velvet Nell, keep your ears and eyes open. Concentrate now, this is really important!'

Isaac, who is so absentminded he is rarely trusted with real tasks, was thrilled. He scampered away, towards the stage door. I only prayed he would find his way to Charing Cross Road. Meanwhile Waldo and I continued down the passageway. We both noticed a sign which said: 'PROPS' at the same time, and simultaneously broke into a run.

Waldo made it just before me. He opened the door, revealing a large space filled with the most incredible collection of junk. Right in front of us was a table, set as if for afternoon tea with white lace doilies and china cups and saucers. There was a big gold and glass case, bound all over and secured with a stout padlock. A stuffed monkey, two dogs and a parrot. A large hanging depicting Venus rising out of the waves. A dolphin modelled from clay, identical to the one in the wings, except this one had a large crack in its head.

'How are we going to find anything among this rubbish?' I groaned.

'Let's do this properly,' Waldo suggested. 'I'll start at the back. You keep a look-out.'

'No! I'll do the searching, Waldo.'

'Bossed by a chit of a girl! The way you talk to me you'd *think* I was the younger one!'

I was tempted to point out that Waldo was only older than me by a few months. Anyway, girls are certainly more mature than boys, but I didn't want to annoy him.

'Keeping a look-out is more dangerous. I'm scared to hang about in this dark passage by myself.'

Waldo looked suspicious; he guessed he was being tricked, but reluctantly agreed. I nipped back into the props room, turned on a lamp and began searching from the back. Oh it was a hopeless task! Finding a pearl in the sea would be easier. Everything was a mess. A pile of painted canvas scenes and ballet girl props under the tiny window. I was holding up a long, thin pole with a hoop on the top and wondering what on earth it could be for when Waldo dived back into the room with an urgent cry.

'Hide! Quick!'

I turned off the lamp. We dived into the same place, behind a bookcase filled with leather-bound volumes. A few fell on the floor. They were fake, blocks of wood painted to look like books.

'I'm all done in. Why has it gotta be tonight, Barney?'

Peeping out through a chink in the bookcase I could see the speaker was a stocky man in a yellow jersey. Another man strolled in. His performer's stockings peeped out underneath a velvet dressing gown trimmed with gold braid. Everything about him – from the way he sat down on an upturned box, to the time he took replying to the question while he puffed slowly on his cigar – was arrogant.

'That's what 'Er Majesty wants. Never question orders if you wanna get ahead in this game.'

'We're fagged out. Me head hurts. Me knees 'ave got cramp. I bin up slavin' on this 'ere show since –'

'Nell doesn't give a hoot about your knees,' Barney replied. I realised he was the acrobat who'd impersonated the Prince of Wales though he looked very different now he'd removed his false whiskers.

'Where's it orf to then?'

'Baker Brothers want it. Round at 101 Eaton Square, Mayfair. Use the tradesmen's entrance.'

'The Baker Brothers?' the stagehand's voice dropped

in awe and I felt my own heart miss a beat. I must have misheard. It couldn't be right, not *the* Baker Brothers!

'Them swells.'

'Everyone is swells to the likes of you.'

'Wot do they want wiv a 'orrible old stinkin' mummy?'

'Did yer go to school?' Barney's voice had dropped to a menacing murmur.

'No, Barney.'

'Do yer know how to read and write?'

'No.'

'Do we pay you to think? Or do we pay yer to use those big, stupid muscles to move things?'

'Er . . .'

'We pay you for your muscles, you glocky moron. If we wanted brains we'd hire a professor. So stop boring me to me grave and get a move on!'

Barney obviously saw *himself* as the brains. He didn't exert himself at all. He stretched back, puffing out a cloud of smoke, while the poor stagehand frantically jumped to attention, moving the clutter of props about in his search for the mummy. Finally, I could see, he unearthed a box, about the same shape and size as the original mummy case. The man opened it up and Barney strolled over and took a look inside.

'That's all in order. Yer can load it up,' Barney said.

'There's a hansom carriage waiting outside. Can you manage it yerself?'

The man tried. He lifted it up, till his muscles stood out like knots of oak. It was no good, the packing case was simply too large and unwieldy.

'All right,' Barney lazily strolled out of the door. We heard a piercing whistle and a moment later who should appear in the room but our old friend Jabber.

'Get this out of 'ere. Sharpish,' Barney ordered.

'Righto, Bender!' Jabber said.

'Oi! How many times 'ave I told yer not to call me by that name!' Barney gave Jabber a smack round the ear. 'Get a move on, yer insolent toad.'

Jabber kept his mouth shut after that, which must have been an effort. Together the man and the boy shifted the packing case to the door and then disappeared down the corridor.

Meanwhile, crouched behind the bookcase in a position which made my calves ache I was falling victim to a fresh bout of despair. We'd been so close! In another few minutes I might have found the mummy. Now it was gone. Out of our reach.

I had failed, again.

I was getting a bad case of cramp in this tight, airless space. Waldo, who is quite a bit taller than I, looked even more squashed than I felt. I hoped that the loathsome

'Bender' Barney would go away, leaving us free to try and follow the hansom cab with the mummy. But not a bit of it. While we struggled to breathe, he sat on his box, puffing away, carefree and apparently deep in thought. He looked like he'd settled down for a good, long smoke.

Suddenly Waldo sneezed. It sounded like a box of fireworks exploding.

'Rats in the wainscoting, eh?' Lazily Barney arose from the case and paced towards us.

I curled myself against the wall, willing Waldo to remain silent with all my might.

'I don't remember no rodents in 'ere,' Barney said to himself. Did he know where we were? He was almost upon us, then at the last moment he turned to the left and pushed aside a large case. I saw him look behind the case and then, disappointed, move away. Still puffing away on his cigar, he began to pace silently up and down the small space in the centre of the room. We held our breaths. Then, as if the movement exhausted him, he sat down again on his box and flicked the stump of his cigar on the floor.

'No one likes vermin,' Barney said. 'Human-shaped, animal-shaped or vermin-shaped.'

Abruptly, he stood up. He was looking straight at us. Had we made a noise? Something was glinting in his hand as he stalked up to the bookcase, reached behind it and pulled me out, Waldo stumbling after me.

'Kids.' Barney looked us over in disgust. 'Wot are yer? Stagehands or what? Scarper or I'll call the manager.' The glinting thing in his hand was a peashooter, a tiny pistol no bigger than a lady's fist.

We 'scarpered'. Waldo dashing off first. We had almost made it to the door when Barney swore. His hand stretched out and grabbed me from behind by my shoulder. My blouse ripped, leaving a strip of cloth in the thug's hand.

'Hold up. Turn round. You ain't the kids Velvet Nell's got a bee in her bonnet about, are you? She got the whole family searching for the little rats who've bin hanging around Zwinglers. Blooming hell, I'll bet you are. I recognise the description. Girl who acts like a lad, that's what she said. All right, hands up, I'm taking you straight to Nell.'

The peashooter was pointed at my chest. Poised to blow a perfect hole through my heart. I raised my hands above my head. The shame of it was I couldn't stop them trembling.

A leer splitting his lips, the acrobat walked up to me, till he was an inch from my face. He smelt foul. He placed the gun against my neck. My breath caught in my throat, muscles seizing up all the way to my stomach. Barney could see my fear and he enjoyed it. He was smiling. *Smiling.*

❧ Chapter Fifteen ❧

'You two will be fish-food before the sun rises.'

Bender moved the barrel of the pistol along my neck. I couldn't feel anything, except the gun, cold against my skin. Finally, after what seemed an age, he took it away and I could breathe again.

'See, Nell don't know the meaning of mercy. Ask her what the word means. Go on, give it a try. She'll probably think it's a new kind of ladies' fashion,' the man assumed an odious falsetto voice: '"The Mercy Corset Essential for all Ladies of Taste and Refinement."'

Keeping his eyes on us, Bender Barney lounged back against the wall, the deadly toy in his hand covering us both. Without the whiskers he'd worn in his disguise as the Prince of Wales there was a repulsive weakness in his chin. His tiny mouth disappeared into folds of fat, seeming almost to merge with his neck.

'Never seen Nell so angry. Well, not since last yesterday. Said you lot are toffs. Pokin' around where you're not wanted.'

'You've got the wrong children, sir,' I managed to stutter. 'We're just stagehands.'

As soon as I'd uttered a word I realised I'd done the wrong thing. My voice bred in Oxford had given me away. Barney would realise instantly that I was no street urchin.

'You've got the wrong children, sir!' Viciously Barney mocked my accent. 'Thank you, your ladyship. You've saved us a lot of bother, coming here nice and easy. Lambs to the slaughter, that's wot I say. Look sharp. Out, quick.' Waving the gun, he directed us out of the door.

I could take nothing in. Make no plans. I felt sick, my brain aflame with fevered thoughts. It was I who had planned this silly escapade. It would all be my fault if we were murdered and – as Barney promised – bundled into the Thames.

An explosion cut through me. Followed by an awful rattling. I turned, startled.

Waldo and Barney were intertwined, a flailing mass of arms and legs. For a moment I could make no sense of it at all. Then I saw Barney firing his gun, while Waldo struggled to catch his hand. Bang, a bullet ricocheted off a tin picture of the Duke of Wellington. I stood and stared, like a fool. What was wrong with me? I felt sluggish. As if wading through treacle.

Waldo struck Barney hard on the chest, cutting off his breath. Barney retaliated with a nasty kick at Waldo's knee. The pea-shooter was firing wildly, a stream of bullets zinging crazily through the room. I snapped to and ran to them. Jumping up I tried to grab the gun.

'Don't be an idiot,' Waldo roared. 'You'll be shot.'

He landed an uppercut to Barney's jaw. The thug's head flopped to the side. I kicked him and Waldo followed up with a punch in his chest. Bender sagged, slumping to the floor in a heap of satin and velvet.

'Oh . . .' I gasped and couldn't go on, my breathing was so painful. I stood in the doorway, trembling.

Waldo regarded me for an instant, eyes blazing. He was furious. 'I –' he began and stopped. Abruptly he turned away: 'Better make a run for it. Before he comes round.'

I followed Waldo down the corridor, feeling very shaky. I was ashamed of my pathetic behaviour. I, who had always prided myself on being different from the Minchin and the other fools who fainted at the hint of blood. Instead of being brave I had turned into jelly. Was it fear that made me react so feebly? I was ashamed of myself.

'Get a hold of yourself, Kit,' Waldo turned round, breaking into my reverie. I'd realised I had come to a standstill. 'We have to be quick.'

We skirted our way through a maze of corridors, till we found signs for the stage door. The people we passed paid us no heed. Then we tumbled out of the theatre into the chill night air of a back alley. Straight into fog. As thick as wood smoke, it curled along the alley, reducing visibility to a couple of yards. Through the murk we could see the outlines of a couple of loungers, the shadows of a few horses further down. No sign of a hansom carriage. Infuriatingly the mummy must already be well on its way to the Baker Brothers' home. It was very late, nearly midnight by Waldo's pocket watch.

We crept down the alley into the fairytale world of Leicester Square. The blazing front of the Alhambra competed with the illuminations of the Turkish Baths next door. Some instinct made me tug Waldo back. He had been about to step into the arc of gaslight. A moment later I spotted some familiar faces, shining sickly greenish-grey through the fog. The Velvet Mob. Among them, looking very grey indeed, was Barney. How had he recovered so quickly? Maybe he was a magician as well as an acrobat. There was a huge commotion in front of the theatre. Several of the mob were shouting. In the midst of them I had a glimpse of Nell in a scarlet cloak, her lily-white face furious. A shiver went through me, I would not want to be one of her gang tonight.

We had an advantage over the hoodlums. London was on our side. Under cover of the smog, we made our way; keeping out of lamp-lit streets, taking comfort from the shadows of the towering buildings. We came into Charing Cross Road and I spotted our friend. For once he had done as he was told and was waiting outside a bookseller's. Isaac is not a patient boy. He was wriggling around on the pavement as if he had ants in his shirt.

A carriage clipped towards us and a friendly driver peered down from the cab.

'Want a ride 'ome, miss?'

I glanced at Waldo. We had just enough money for the fare and we were both exhausted.

'Thanks, cabbie.' Waldo scrambled in and I followed. I was just about to request the driver to stop for Isaac when I felt a pressure on my arm. Someone was squeezing me roughly. I turned, about to protest when my words died on my lips. Looming out of the shadows was a familiar face. Those repulsive lips, merging smoothly into the chin. Those malicious, piggy eyes.

Bender Barney! How had he come to be sitting in the back of this cab?

'Hello, me lovely.' He grinned and lifted one hand lazily, the fabric of my blouse dangled from his fingers.

Bender was covering Waldo with his pistol. How

could we have been so stupid? We'd handed ourselves to the Velvet Mob. On a platter.

Isaac. At least he had a chance. I leaned forward, sticking my head out of the doorway and screamed at my friend on the pavement below. 'Run, Isaac. Run. They've got us!' was all I managed before Bender removed his hand from Waldo's mouth and clapped it over mine.

Isaac looked up at me startled, still wriggling about crazily. His eyes met mine. Then he moved. A streak sped across the deserted street, faster than anyone could run. An illusion almost, a smooth blur of matter and light. Grazing the horses noses as it zoomed past.

The horses went wild, rearing up in alarm. The cab toppled to the side. Panic blossomed inside me. I was dimly aware of trampling horses, firing guns, bodies falling heavily against me. The window smashed into a hundred glittering pieces. A shard of glass speared Bender's top hat, close to taking out his eye. His hand fell, and his gun dropped to the floor. I grabbed part of the window frame and bashed Bender on the head.

'Take that!' I screamed.

'STOP!' Waldo hollered, pulling me away. 'We've got to get out of here.'

We scrambled out of the destroyed cab. Waldo's shoulder was bleeding where a piece of glass had pierced it. Where was Isaac? Over there, on the other side of the road. We ran to him and scooped him up, thankful he had not been trampled by the rearing horses. One of them, a majestic black gelding, was neighing horribly.

'What happened?' I hissed at Isaac as we hastened down a side alley, away from the wreck and the thug's pursuit.

For an answer he paused for a fraction of a second and lifted his right foot. In a flash he was gone down the alley, a smooth blur of navy blue coat and flickering legs on those magical wheels. So that was what had startled the horses: Isaac's crazy invention. We ran after him, Waldo struggling to keep up with me as blood poured down his jacket from his wounded shoulder. Panting, we came to a stop by a grinning Isaac.

'What on earth?' I asked him.

'RollerShoes.' He smiled at me. 'Told you they'd come in handy.'

'More than handy, Isaac. They saved our lives.'

❧ Chapter Sixteen ❧

It was middle of the day after our adventure at the Alhambra and Waldo was still in bed. He lay in state on his throne of fluffy pillows, surrounded by fruit and flowers, sipping a glass of lime cordial that Aunt's cook had specially prepared for him. There were so many bandages around his upper arm they formed a lump under his striped nightgown. He looked like a hunch-shoulder, if such a thing exists.

'Oh come on,' I cajoled him. 'It can't be that bad.'

'You always make light of things when they happen to *me*,' he said pettishly.

'A piece of glass pierced your skin,' I snapped. 'You weren't stabbed nearly to death like Baruch.'

'Your precious greener. It's all very well to coddle him, but with me it's all just a joke.'

'Come on, you two,' Rachel intervened gently. 'I'm sure Kit doesn't want to make light of your pain, Waldo. Can we do anything to make you more comfortable?'

Rather grumpily, Waldo admitted he had everything he needed. I should think so! He was as cosseted as a little maharajah. In fact he had me to thank for all this. If I hadn't come up with a story to explain his wounded shoulder – a rather improbable one, I admit, involving a broken glass of water – he would be in serious trouble. In the event all the servants were fluttering around him as if he was a hero of the Crimean war.

Waldo tended to have that effect on servants. Especially the prettier maids.

'We're going to visit the hospital,' Rachel went on. 'Ahmed is staying here. We really think we should see if Baruch is all right –' she flashed me a look. 'Especially as Kit got him into this mess.'

I knew Waldo. He hated to miss an adventure, but even he could not suddenly claim to be better. We left him moaning that girls had all the fun these days – though I can't see how a visit to a hospital can be described as *fun*. Two omnibus rides later we were at Charing Cross Hospital, which is a modern place, known for the quality of its care. A nurse directed us to Baruch's ward, up several flights of steps, near the top of the building.

When I entered the ward I thought there was some mistake. That I had been directed to a morgue. It was a large, gloomy room, with bare boards stacked with iron cots. The half-dead were all around us. Men with whooping cough, spluttering away. Others so thin from consumption they looked like living skeletons. The air was sour with boiled cabbage and disease, thick with coughs and groans. No one had thought to open the small window, set high up in the wall, to bring some air into this misery. In the far corner we spotted Baruch, wrapped in as many bandages as a mummy. With some trepidation we made our way over to him. He seemed surprised, but I think pleased, to see us. We gave him our gifts and sat chatting for a while, though we could see every word cost him an effort. Then looking at the ceiling he said something that made my heart wrench:

'If I stay here I die.'

'No –' I began but Baruch cut me off.

'I don't say this to beg for your pity. I say because it is fact.'

His filthy curls were stuck to his face with sweat, his face drained of blood. I knew there was truth in his words. I would rather recover from an illness in a pigsty than in this place. Surely someone had understood that packing the diseased so close together, like pieces of kindling in a fire, was unhealthy? Surely someone had thought of the benefits of clean air? The only bit of colour in the whole room was the posy of flowers Rachel and I had brought for Baruch. Along with some juicy apples, they rested on the floor by Baruch's bed. He wouldn't find it till later, but nestling under the fruit was a guinea, which I had managed to beg from Aunt Hilda.

"'Ow's our patient today?' A nurse stopped at our bedside. She was friendly and smiling, but the wares on her trolley looked awful. She ladled soup out of a steaming pot into an enamel bowl and handed it to Baruch. A watery concoction of cabbage and gristle.

'Got a treat in store for you today. Some tasty sheep's brains in the pot. Tuck in, me dear.'

I took the bowl and set it carefully on the floor, by the flowers.

'Make sure you eat it while it's 'ot,' the nurse called as she went on to the next patient. 'Gets 'orrible lumpy when it's cold.'

All around the room, to my astonishment, men were eating the gruel with every sign of enjoyment.

Baruch couldn't stay here. The food would kill him if the infection in the air didn't. Would it be any better at the sweatshop though? I glanced at Rachel. Could we somehow persuade Aunt Hilda to let Baruch stay?

'It is no matter. I will go back to Zwinglers,' Baruch said as if he could read my mind. 'Sara will bring me there in a cab. It is costly but she says I cannot go in omnibus.'

'We can lend you some money.'

'I am your cause, eh? Charity of the week.'

'It isn't like that,' I said, embarrassed. I was so much younger than Baruch, but here I was offering him help. I could understand if he resented it. 'I dragged you into this mess. You got stabbed because of us, Baruch. Paying for your cab is the least we can do.'

'We're worried about you,' Rachel put in. 'Will you be all right at the shop?'

Baruch shrugged, a painful movement in all those bandages. 'Moses is hard. But not a monster. He will let me rest till I am better and –'

'Then what?' I asked, but Baruch was no longer listening. For there behind us was Sara. What a transformation! Her dark curls were brushed and glossy. Dressed in a rose-coloured blouse and skirt, she looked shyly pretty. A different girl from the downtrodden drab we had seen at Zwinglers. She approached the bed slowly. Baruch heaved himself up on one elbow and took her hand.

'You are beautiful.'

Sara flushed becomingly.

'I tell them.'

The girl didn't answer, her cheeks were still suffused with colour and she was looking down at the grimy floor as if too embarrassed to meet Baruch's eyes.

'We marry. As soon as I become well,' Baruch said.

'Wonderful! Congratulations!' Rachel and I burst out. Baruch silenced us.

'We married and then we go!'

'Where?' Rachel asked.

'To the new world.'

'America,' I breathed.

'Yes. Sara and I have money for our ticket to New York. I have no dreams. America will be hard, like London. But I want to breathe.'

'Work,' Sara put in.

'Yes. Work. Not be slaves. We will work hard and who knows, we hope God will bless us. We want walk free and proud. In our new world.' The effort of talking so much had cost Baruch. He sank back on to the bed, a little white froth on his lips. Rachel looked at me. We should leave them, her glance said, but I pressed on for there was something I had to know.

'We've tracked down the Velvet Mob. I've met Jabber Jukes.'

'Jabber.' Baruch glared up at the cracked ceiling as if it was his enemy.

'I'm aware he's a little monster but we've learnt some very interesting things about the Velvet Mob. We nearly found our mummy, only, well, we blew it. Thing is, we overheard the villains saying they're taking it to 101 Eaton Square. The Baker Brothers' house. Except that can't be true . . .'

I thought a moment, struggling to summarise what I knew about the Brothers. They were the picture of respectability, always dressed in identical dark suits, their blonde hair combed in the same way. The Brothers had spent a fortune giving away chocolate, tea and coffee to working folk. They were famous campaigners against alcohol – wanted to provide an alternative to gin – which they hated for the ruin it brought to families. The thing was impossible. True, not much was known about them. They were very reclusive and almost never appeared in public. Still, they were admired all over the Empire for good works.

'I know the Baker Brothers, at least my aunt does,' I continued. 'They're friends of the Prince of Wales. They can't be mixed up in all this thieving and –'

I stopped abruptly, realising that I was blabbering. Baruch had frozen in his recumbent position. His grip on Sara's hand was so tight, I could see he was hurting her. He spoke a few words to her which I didn't understand. His fiancée helped him up, propping him against the hard iron bed-head. Baruch looked at both of us in turn, his brown eyes full of fear.

'I warn you. You *must* listen. This Velvet Mob is wicked thing. They beat. They rob. They belong in jail. But the Baker Brothers. We know the truth in Petticoat

Lane. We do not believe what the world thinks. We know. They are –' he paused and his eyes flashed as he said something to Rachel – a word that was an unpronounceable mixture of sounds . . . something like 'tayvolim'.

Rachel looked troubled for a second and then turned to me: 'Devil. Baruch says they are fiends, devils.'

'Devils,' Baruch nodded. 'Devils clothed in human flesh.'

A glimmer of an idea rose in my mind and I looked at Rachel excitedly. 'I know, I've got an idea about how we can find them and –'

Baruch interrupted me: 'Please, please, my friend. Stay away from these men.'

I shifted uncomfortably, unable to look him in the eye.

'You must understand. The Baker Brothers are too powerful for you to fight.'

❧ Chapter Seventeen ❧

'I'm not intimidated,' I said. 'The Baker Brothers can't scare *me* off.'

'Hot air,' Rachel snapped. 'I don't think two of the richest men in the Empire are going to lose sleep over a twelve-year-old.'

We had all gathered in my aunt's library for a conference. The sun slanting through tall windows onto wood panelling and rows of leather-bound books provided a soothing atmosphere. It hadn't soothed us, though. We were in the middle of a full-blown row. I was all for turning up at the Baker Brothers' house, seeing if we could somehow gain admittance, and then searching the place for the mummy. Rachel, reasonably enough I suppose, pointed out that we were not trained burglars. If Baruch was right, the Brothers were vicious. We had to be careful.

'Listen here, Ahmed,' I said turning to our Egyptian friend. 'There's something I don't understand. Why do the Baker Brothers want this mummy so much? I mean there are thousands of mummies in Egypt.'

Ahmed hesitated, searching for the words in English probably: 'Ptah Hotep was a holy man. A vizier to the king.'

'Was it the scarab?' Waldo suggested. 'Do they know about the scarab?'

'Maybe,' Ahmed replied.

'Another thing that has puzzled me,' I said to Ahmed. 'Why didn't you get the scarab yourself, when you were trapped in the ship's hold with the mummy?'

'It was not possible. You saw how hard the sarcophagus was to open in your Aunt Hilda's play. And that was after the thieves had already stolen Ptah Hotep's mummy, broken into the case, once before. I had no axe or such things when I was trapped.'

I fell silent, musing. We were on the verge of something, I could feel it. Abruptly, Isaac, who had been immersed in a book in the corner of the library, spoke. 'Ptah Hotep. The mummy. He's in the centre of this somehow. We have to find out more about him.' He advanced towards us, carrying a large book titled:

A SURVEY OF EGYPTOLOGY FROM THE OLD TO NEW KINGDOMS

'Look,' Isaac pointed out a paragraph in the book. For the benefit of Ahmed, who of course could not understand written English, I read it out:

'All the signs are that King Djedkare Isesi of the fifth dynasty enjoyed a long and stable rule. Manetho, the Greek historian, says he was pharaoh for forty-five years, though other sources give him a shorter reign.'

'What's the point of this?' Waldo interrupted.

'Hold on,' I snapped.

A collection of sayings by the legendary royal councillor Ptah Hotep, were found in Thebes, Egypt by the French archaeologist Prisse D'Avennes. This papyrus is believed to be at least two thousand years old and is a copy of an even older original. Of course we do not know what the original papyrus contained, it has long been lost. But the surviving sayings are remarkable, covering everything from the art of ruling a kingdom to how to treat women. They give us a genuine insight into life in Egypt over four thousand years ago.

'Interesting about his collection of sayings,' I remarked. 'But I don't see how it gets us any further.'

'It doesn't,' Waldo said decisively. 'All we really know

is that the Baker Brothers have the mummy of Ptah Hotep, which contains a malachite heart scarab. They really, really want it for some secret reason. Tried to buy it from your aunt, and when that failed they had it stolen. Let's stick to facts. The rest is sheer guesswork.'

'I'm with Waldo,' I said. 'The Bakers have the mummy and the scarab. What we need is a plan. A clever way to get into their house and find them!'

'I could try one of my inventions,' Isaac suggested, but his words were soon drowned by a chorus of groans.

'Unless we can find that mummy,' I continued, 'we're sunk. We won't be able to save the scarab and, more importantly, your father's life.' I turned to Ahmed.

My words hung in the air. I looked at my friends in turn and I must say my spirits did not lift. Certainly, Waldo was brave, a good fighter to have by one's side. Isaac was clever, in a somewhat scatterbrained way, and very inventive. And Rachel. Poor old Rachel, good-hearted for sure, but otherwise not much use. As for Ahmed, he was a foreigner, how could he be expected to take on the wicked Baker Brothers? So, as usual, it was down to me to think of a plan.

I paced up and down in the library, my thoughts travelling faster than a steam train. Should we start a fire at the Bakers' house and try and sneak in under cover of the chaos? Disguise ourselves as butcher's boys and seek entrance to the Brothers' kitchen? Could I try to obtain a job, as a scullery maid for instance, at the house?

No, all these ideas were unlikely to bear fruit. Then I thought of something that made me clap my hands in glee. So simple it was sure to work.

'We're not going to sneak into the Bakers' mansion like a lot of thieves in the night,' I said.

'Certainly not,' Rachel agreed.

'We'll walk right in.' I announced. 'We'll walk in through the front door as honoured guests!'

'How?' the others chorused. 'That won't work . . . they'll throw us straight out!' Even Rachel, who is all for doing things the proper way, looked unconvinced.

'Patience.' I grinned. 'You lot of unbelievers will just have to wait and see what Kit cooks up!'

101 Eaton Square was an imposing cream-coloured mansion set behind tall iron railings. It had seven floors that towered into the sky and was adorned with a pattern of foliage and leaves around the windows that looked Roman. The large, curved windows were protected by iron bars, a gleaming brass knocker was set against the black front door.

My aunt marched up the steps to the door, Isaac and Ahmed and I trailing after her. That's right. I took the simplest way of penetrating the Baker Brothers mansion. My aunt had boasted of her friendship with the Brothers, so I'd suggested to her that she seek their help in finding her mummy. Who knows, I'd told her, the millionaire businessmen might even fund her next expedition.

Aunt Hilda, preoccupied with finding supporters in her battle against the French, had taken the bait straight away. It seems the reclusive Brothers were known for their patriotism, so my aunt was hopeful that they might come to her aid. It was a simple matter to attach ourselves to her coat-tails. But she had laid down one condition: she wouldn't take more than two or three of us. Despite his bitter protests, Waldo, who was still complaining of his shoulder injury, was left at home with Rachel.

That would teach him not to make such a fuss about a simple cut!

A butler in black coat and tails appeared in answer to my aunt's knock. Bowing, he ushered us in and soon we were divested of our coats and waiting in a gloomy room, which had a view of a long corridor, with a number of doors leading off it. Opposite us was a brass plaque which read LIBRARY. I would have loved to sneak off in there, see what secrets the Bakers were hiding, but with my aunt around I had to watch my step.

Important people like to keep you waiting. We had been sitting in the dusty and sunless parlour for at least half an hour, while my aunt moaned and groaned and paced around restlessly. Finally the door to the library opened and a little man slipped out. I caught a glimpse of the Baker Brothers, sitting behind the largest desk I've ever seen. They were wearing identical suits, in a creamy fabric, their light hair parted in the same way. With their long, miserable faces they looked like a pair of bled horses.

Or ghosts. There was something sinister about the way they appeared suddenly out of the gloom. They seemed insubstantial. After all, like ghosts there wasn't a single picture of the Baker Brothers in existence. They never appeared in public but drifted behind the scenes, pulling strings. They weren't seen at the usual haunts of millionaires, they had no box at the opera, did not frequent Mayfair balls or soirées at Buckingham Palace. Some people even went so far as to claim they didn't exist.

'Miss Hilda Salter?' the little man said, approaching my aunt. Then his eye fell on Ahmed, Isaac and I. 'Goodness! What is this?'

'Don't worry, they're house-trained,' Aunt Hilda said gaily.

'An absolute gaggle of little creatures.' He peered at us, horrified. 'What are they?'

'Who are they, you mean. My niece Kit and her chums, amateur archaeologists.'

'No. They absolutely cannot come in. The Brothers cannot bear children. They positively loathe the messy, loud, brainless little goblins.'

'Fine,' my aunt said, standing up. 'Children, you will wait for me here.'

The little man glared at us as he ushered my aunt into the Brothers' presence: 'No snooping!'

'Let's snoop,' Isaac said as the door banged shut after them. 'Where do you think these thugs keep their secrets?'

The corridor stretched endlessly. The walls were lined with portraits, an exceedingly ugly collection of ancestors, if that is what they were. There was a bewildering number of doors.

'Which one do you think we should try?' Isaac continued.

'That one,' I said, pointing to the door next to the library, which bore a plaque marked STUDY. 'Something tells me it's the study.'

The room was richly decorated, the walls lined with paintings, including one famous Italian painting which I had seen somewhere before. A lady with a mysterious smile, in front of a hazy vista of hills. Had I read somewhere that this particular painting had been stolen?

There were no bookshelves, but inserted in the wall was a massive safe built by Mr Chubb, who boasted his locks were unpickable. Isaac, of course, was instantly drawn to the safe.

The desk was absolutely clean, except for one manuscript. Annoyingly, the drawers were locked.

'There's nothing here,' I said, frustrated, bending down to the carpet to search for some forgotten slip of paper which might give us the clue we needed. Where, oh, where were the Brothers keeping the mummy? 'These men are so clean and tidy it can't be true.'

Isaac, who had given up on the safe, picked up the manuscript on the desk and gave a low whistle. 'What do you make of this?' he asked, passing it to me. It was a copy of my father's latest book, *The World's Oldest Words: from the Book of the Dead to the Rig Veda*. It hadn't even been published. My father had spent three years working on the book and was terribly proud of it, but no one except a handful of learned men could be expected to read it. How had the Baker Brothers got hold of it?

'It doesn't make sense,' Isaac said. 'Why would they want this?'

'Who knows?' I replied, my attention diverted by a small door, opposite the Chubb safe. I approached the door and turned the handle, to my delight it opened into a room the size of a cubby-hole. It was in total darkness.

I tiptoed over to the window, almost stumbling over something on the floor and opened the shutters, letting sunlight flood in.

Isaac and Ahmed had joined me. What we saw lying on the parquet floor made us gasp. A pile of bandages thrown in a disorderly heap. Next to them, a shrunken, gnarled old thing. It reminded me of the roots of an ancient, blackened tree. No, that wasn't quite right. There was something leathery about the mummy, something shiny and almost translucent. Like a strip of skin peeled off your thumb.

I identified the sharp, citrus scent in the air as natron, the salt used by the embalmers all those millennia ago to preserve the corpse. Kneeling down by it, I took a closer look. You could still see the shape of Ptah Hotep's cheek, the blackened and decayed teeth. Even a few wisps of reddish hair adhering to the four-thousand-year-old skull. The mummy's empty eye sockets seemed to peer out at me from across the ages.

A hush fell over us as we gazed at the mummy. The ancient sage, Ptah Hotep looked back at us, over the chasm of the ages. A miracle of miracles.

All was not well with the mummy. Of course there was the ancient damage to the corpse. The slit in his side, where the embalmers had removed the internal organs. But that was a neat cut and it had been sewn up.

What angered me was the evidence of more recent violence to his person. One side of Ptah Hotep's rib cage had been brutally bashed in. His neck was broken. It was cruel. Sheer vandalism. Ahmed, by my side, made a furious noise in his throat. His eyes had a wild glitter.

'How could they do this to him?' he hissed. 'They are savages. No respect.'

'Shush,' I quietened Ahmed. 'We must be calm.'

'They don't care about the mummy,' Isaac said softly. 'It is not what they are after.'

'They don't care about anything,' Ahmed spat.

I was searching in the pile of bandages, but already I knew the truth. The scarab was not there.

'The Baker Brothers found the scarab. That's all they want.' Ahmed said. 'They have no idea of what is good or holy or true. No respect for anything. All they know is what they desire. These men, they want the scarab. They find it so they have no care for this gentle man's soul. They, how do you say, they smash Ptah Hotep.' It was one of the longest speeches I'd heard him utter. The blood had drained from his face but he spoke calmly.

'The scarab has gone, Ahmed.' I said, rising from the heap of bandages. 'Look, we won't have much time. Isaac, can you get into the safe? I bet the scarab's in there.'

We went into the next room and stared at the safe. It

167

was an impressive object, a glittering combination of black enamel and bronze. The lock looked impregnable.

'Can you get into that, Isaac?' I repeated.

'I'll give it a go,' Isaac replied, but he sounded doubtful.

Suddenly there was a noise of scraping from the room next door. 'Quick,' I hissed. We scampered out of the room, down the corridor and into the waiting room. We just had time to return to our seats before the secretary opened the door and ushered my aunt out. He cast a suspicious look at my flushed face:

'Where's the other one?' the secretary said.

'Pardon.'

'The thin one. The one with dirty hair and glasses.'

With a stab of horror I realised that Isaac had not made it back to our seats. The foolish boy had vanished. Really he was more of a liability than anything. I had to think fast.

'I'm afraid my friend has had to rush home,' I lied, hoping my 'innocent' face was convincing. 'He suffers from a serious vomiting illness and didn't want to be sick on the rugs.'

'What's this illness called?' the secretary asked, still frowning.

I was straining to come up with a name for his fictitious disease, when to my surprise Aunt Hilda joined in with the deception. 'You mean Isaac's bilharzia?' she said.

'He caught it in China, poor boy. His vomit is green when he really gets going and they say it's terribly catching.'

Involuntarily, the secretary shuddered and drew back from us. There was a definite haste in the way he led us down to the lobby and out of the door. I had the feeling he was glad to be rid of us. Out in Eaton Square my aunt strode ahead of us, I had to run to keep up.

'Thanks, Aunt Hilda,' I muttered.

'I don't know what you are up to Kit and to be candid, I don't want to know,' she replied.

'But what on earth is bilharzia?'

'Haven't a clue,' she replied airily. 'Probably a type of rum from Rangoon.'

I gaped at Aunt Hilda. 'It was decent of you to help us out.'

'I couldn't bear to let that odious little man get the better of you. You must learn to keep a straight face when you're telling fibs, my dear. The secret of successful lying is all in the delivery.'

My aunt settled herself in the waiting carriage, arranging her carpet bag and umbrella to her satisfaction on the leather seat. Ahmed and I squeezed ourselves into the remaining space. I was thinking of requesting that we wait for Isaac but Aunt Hilda had already boomed a command to the driver. We were off, the horses threading their way through the heavy West

End traffic. There was a set look on my aunt's face, as she gazed out of the window. I wondered if her mission was a success, but instinct told me to hold my tongue. If she had received bags of sovereigns from the Baker Brothers she would be boasting about it.

Discretion was definitely the best policy with Aunt Hilda, when she was in this mood. As her carriage made its way back to Bloomsbury, we sat in silence. I was sick with anxiety about Isaac. If he was caught by the Bakers' thugs snooping in their house, they would not be gentle with him. The secretary might very well check with the butler and find out that my friend had not left the house. Isaac was a dreamer, a thinker. Not someone suited to safe-breaking. He wouldn't know what a 'jemmy' was, not if it hit him square on the head.

At this very moment, while we travelled home to Bloomsbury in safety, for all I knew my friend was being roughed up by thugs. They might shove him in the coal cellar – or, worse, in the Thames. Why had I asked him to break into the safe? But for once I refused to blame myself, not totally anyway. Was it my fault that Isaac displayed the common sense of a flea? Then another thought struck me, one that chilled me to my very bones.

Rachel. What would she have to say about this?

❧ Chapter Seventeen ❧

I opened the door to the parlour, weary and depressed. Sitting on the maroon velvet sofa, deep in conversation, looking solid and real were my father and Isaac. I blinked in surprise. I was seeing things. I must be seeing things. Isaac was back at the Bakers' mansion, being torn limb-from-limb by their thugs, and my father was in Oxford. I was about to retreat to my room for a good, baffled lie-down when my aunt barged in behind me.

'Good afternoon, Theo,' she bellowed as my father stood up to greet us. Then she turned to Isaac. 'And – you, fellow! How d'ya get here before us?'

'I took an omnibus,' Isaac replied calmly, as if he was a real flesh-and-blood boy, not a ghost at all.

'Dratted driver. I always tell him not to go via Hyde Park and he always ignores me. Traffic is atrocious round there. The man has no sense.'

With that Aunt Hilda bundled out of the room and clomped down the hall calling for the maid Mary. I sank on the sofa next to Isaac and hissed: 'How did you really get here so soon?'

He grinned at me.

'What were you up to at the Bakers'?'

'I have my secrets,' he replied. 'Just like you.'

'I was worried sick about you, Isaac. I thought they were going to kill you.'

'You worry too much,' he said and turned back to my father, resuming their interrupted conversation. 'Now why did you think the Bakers had a copy of your manuscript?'

'I really cannot say,' my father said, mildly. 'It is rather *flattering*, though. I had not envisaged that there would be such an interest in the *World's Oldest Words*. I really do believe there is increasing popular appetite for serious scholarship.'

'What is your book about, Father?' I asked. 'Is there anything about old Egyptian books? Or Ptah Hotep?'

'Why, of course, Kit. You should know that the Book of the Dead is Egyptian, as are many of the oldest manuscripts in the world. For example the The Maxims of Ptah Hotep. This is an ancient papyrus which, unfortunately, the French have got hold of. A Middle Kingdom copy of wisdom from the Old Kingdom, many, many centuries before. Really rather amazing the way scribes passed the wisdom down for centuries, but unfortunately the oldest papyrus has long been destroyed.'

'Do we know much about it? The Ptah Hotep manuscript.'

'Not much solid information,' Father admitted. 'Ptah Hotep is thick with legend and rumour. The French, obviously, know more but they say that magical –'

'What's this about the French?' interrupted my aunt, who had bustled back into the room followed by Mary with a tray laden with whisky and soda. 'Not that rotter Champlon?'

I quickly distracted her. Once she started on the French, we would have no peace. 'How is it that the Baker Brothers are reckoned as such great collectors, Aunt Hilda? It's not as if they have a museum, or do they?'

'I do not think, my dear, you understand collectors,' Aunt Hilda replied. 'A true collector doesn't buy things to display in a museum. He buys them for himself. So he can keep them – possess them.'

'That's not a collector,' I said. 'That's a miser. To hoard treasures just for yourself.'

'Miser, collector. Let's not split hairs.'

'Beautiful things should be enjoyed by everyone.'

'All that matters in the real world, my child, is who can pay. In England the richest man invariably wins.'

Aunt Hilda poured a glass of lemonade and passed it

to me. Mary had already served her with a strong whisky and soda and was now mixing a drink for my father.

'I don't say I'm fond of the Baker Brothers, though I count them as friends of sorts. Stingy fellows, they are. Count every penny of their money. Refused to give me money today, outright.' My aunt downed her whisky in a few large gulps and indicated to Mary to pour her another one. 'But I do believe, Kit, that in this life you have to be a realist. Money counts, my dear. Brass, doubloons, sovereigns, lucre, gold call it what you will. It's money that gets things done, not ideals or other such nonsense.'

Father made a small noise of protest, his woolly head trembled and his eyes were worried. I felt a gush of love for him. Aunt Hilda might be off, haring round the world in search of lucre but for father ideals would always count for more than mere money. In fact, given a choice between a sack of gold and a worthless old manuscript he would opt for the manuscript every time. He was a hopeless old romantic.

There was a sharp tap on the parlour door and the next moment it swung open. A bronzed and stringy man stood in front of us.

'Madame Salter, I believe?' he inquired.

The man was a strange sight. A combination of battered skin and extreme elegance. His complexion was as worn as an old leather saddle, yet he was beautifully dressed in top hat, waistcoat of shot silk and seamed trousers. Over his lips hung the biggest, waxiest, blackest moustache imaginable. More of a plant than a piece of facial hair. The man must tend it lovingly, watering and feeding it at every meal.

'Gaston Champlon,' said the man, executing a bow which made his moustache tremble.

'You!' Aunt Hilda said. 'This is a surprise, I must say. I had you down as too much of a coward to face me!'

'Outrageous,' Champlon spluttered. 'I am wounded to my 'eart.'

'You have no heart!'

'Madame, I cannot have you telling lies about me in the newspapers.'

My aunt drew herself up, all five foot of her, eyes blazing: 'Lies? Just you wait and see what I have up my sleeve.'

'You need to stop these at once!'

'Never!'

'In that case I need to make my challenge. I cannot fight you, madame, for you are a . . .' the Frenchman paused, surveying my aunt's jodhpurs critically. 'You are called a ledee. So name your man and I will challenge 'im. We fight tomorrow at dawn in 'Ampstead 'Eet'. Pistols or swords. The choice is yours, madame, for I am a master of both.'

This couldn't be. Was this crazy Frenchman actually challenging my aunt to a duel?

'Done!' My aunt hopped from foot to foot, quivering with excitement. 'I thought you would never dare to tangle with me, Champlon. Too much of a scared rabbit –'

'Gaston scared of a ledee! Madame, 'ow dare –'

'We will meet you in Hampstead Heath at first light. My brother will be my standard bearer. I myself will act as his second! The weapon will be pistols!'

'Hilda. Wait!!' my father moaned but neither Gaston nor my aunt took the slightest notice. With another formal bow, the Frenchman retreated from the room. As for me, I was in utter shock. My father could not fight Monsieur Champlon. It would be sheer murder; like challenging a pet hamster to fight a boa constrictor.

'I can't do this.' Father sank into the sofa cushions, as if they could offer him a hiding place.

'Pull yourself together, Theo!' My aunt's gaze swept over my father, taking in his faded tweeds, his woolly hair, his trembling face. 'You're not exactly champion material, I admit. But we must face facts, you're all I've got.'

❧ Chapter Nineteen ❧

First light on Hampstead Heath. Down below, the sun rose over the city spires, painting them gold. Wind swooshed through the leaves; otherwise everything lay silent, suspended. Two lean figures were silhouetted in the murk. One had a soup-strainer moustache, forming a dark question mark in the morning fog. The other seemed frailer, unsure in his gait.

'Your paces, gentlemen!' bellowed one of the seconds – a rather squat figure beside the men.

The two gentlemen bowed, turned their backs and slowly began walking back from each other. I counted with them, my heart thundering. One, two, three, four . . . This couldn't be happening, in the heart of London, the most advanced city in the world. Down in the village of Hampstead were telegraph poles and gas lamps. And here in the swirling fog, a murderous medieval ritual was taking place.

'Take your positions, gentlemen,' my aunt called out.

Rachel clutched my arm. We watched from the shade of a clump of elm trees, my friends and I.

'Do not be alarmed, Kit,' my father whispered in my ear. 'Waldo is a fine young man. He will come through this ordeal splendidly.'

I glowered at him. Since when was Waldo a man? He was a boy. Sure he claimed to be a dab hand at the pistols, but these guns were not shooting blanks. How could my father and aunt put up with this? Naturally my father had jumped at Waldo's offer to fight in his place. As for Aunt Hilda, this was proof she had no conscience at all.

'Are you ready?' her voice sang out.

Courteously, Waldo moved to take off his top hat but Champlon gestured to him to keep it on.

'Take your positions. READY . . . AIM . . . FIRE!'

The bullets exploded, startling a flock of crows, which rose in a storm of black feathers. The sharp tang of cordite filled my nostrils and I was vaguely aware of a bullet streaking through the air, fast and deadly, making straight for one of the men. It sliced clear through him. He fell, clutching at his head. A bullet to the brain.

'Waldo!' I screamed, as I ran towards him, Rachel at my side.

His golden curls were wet, lying dark over his fine face. How instantly life can be shut off. I found myself hugging him, clutching at his shirt. Remorse crashed over me. Why had I allowed this? I should have done something to stop it. I was to blame, I –

'Gerroff me.' He squirmed, struggling away.

Waldo alive and well?

'So you do care, Kit?' His blue eyes shone with amusement.

Drawing back, I saw that Waldo's hat had now fallen on the grass. His new top hat. Straight through the centre was a hole the size of a carrot.

Champlon put his gun back in his holster, work done. He regarded us with a fishy stare: 'You zee now?'

'See what?' Aunt Hilda said, defiantly.

'You zee I mean business.'

My father coughed apologetically. 'We certainly do, Monsieur Champlon.'

There was no sign of the shot from Waldo's gun. He must have missed by a mile.

'Zees was a warning only. I do not shoot children. But madame, if I hear any more lies about me in your newspapers, next time it will be –' Champlon paused. 'Next time it will be ze death!'

The French explorer turned his back on us. Accompanied by his taciturn second he stomped off down the hill, towards the lake which lay before Hampstead village. We watched him go in silence. Even my aunt seemed uncharacteristically subdued.

Or so I hoped. In fact I was giving her more credit for human sympathy than was her due. When Champlon had vanished into the fog, she turned to us. Unbelievably she wore a triumphant air.

'We've really got that French blighter rattled. Next time, my dear boy, you'll show him we mean business!'

❧ Chapter Twenty ❧

'Put your little toys away, Waldo,' I shouted above the deafening rat-a-tat of gunfire. 'You lost. That's all there is to it.'

Waldo's face was shiny with sweat, his blond curls tousled, as he lowered the duelling pistols and glared at me. The figure of Gaston Champlon nailed to the oak tree in my aunt's garden was quite dead; riddled with so many holes, it could have served as a sieve. However, easier to shoot a wooden target than a real live man. Especially if, as Aunt Hilda had belatedly revealed, that man was one of the finest shots in the world.

'Champlon is a champion marksman,' I said more gently. 'There's no need to feel humiliated.'

'Humiliation has nothing to do with it. This is about revenge,' Waldo muttered, before he turned his back on me and carried on his target practice. 'Anyway you're just a girl. I don't expect you to understand.'

'A better shot than you, I bet,' I murmured under my

breath, but I turned away and trudged inside. When would that infuriating American realise that girls were every bit as good as boys? I admit that, at times, I almost liked Waldo. Then he would turn round and treat me with lordly condescension. I was 'just a girl'. I didn't 'understand'. As if I was a pea-brain, someone who couldn't join up my letters or eat my soup without a bib. Yet I was every bit as smart as him. In fact, frankly, I was smarter.

Anyway, I had no time for his foul moods. I needed a bit of quiet to concentrate on our quest for the scarab. I went up to the solitude of Aunt Hilda's library. It was wonderfully peaceful: no Frenchmen here, or Americans who fancied themselves cowboys. I would rest a while in one of the squashy armchairs by the bay window.

It was not to be. Ahmed was curled up in one of the armchairs absorbed in a thick, leather-bound book.

'What are you doing here?' I blurted.

He looked up, startled. Then he blushed to his collar-bone.

'Ahmed?'

Our Egyptian guest hadn't wanted to come with us to Hampstead Heath, claiming he feared guns. Now he gaped at me like a child caught stealing sweets. I took the book from his hands and looked at the title. It was a tome of ancient Egyptian history.

'What have you been reading, Ahmed?'

Something wasn't right. Ahmed was just learning to speak English. As far as we were aware, he didn't even recognise our alphabet. No way could he read a complicated, learned book.

'I was just looking at the pictures.'

'Oh, I see,' I said and handed the book back to him. There wasn't a single picture on the pages he'd been looking at. I needed help with this. Help from someone who wasn't scared of a confrontation. I ran off to fetch Waldo – if nothing else this would serve to distract him from his pistols.

'You've been lying to us, Ahmed,' I said, once we had returned.

The young Egyptian looked at me, his gaze firm and clear. I thought he would deny it, but he nodded.

'You've betrayed our trust,' Waldo said.

'Why? Why have you tricked us?' I couldn't keep my voice steady.

Still Ahmed held his tongue, looking straight at us with that steady, unashamed gaze. It was all coming together in my mind. The unbelievable speed at which he'd learnt English. His sophistication. I was convinced now. Ahmed was not who he claimed to be. Maybe he was actually a treasure hunter. But instead of shrinking and cringing when we confronted him with his treachery, the opposite was happening. He was stretching out, seeming to become taller and more composed.

'Yes,' he said at last. 'I admit it, I lied.'

His accent had dropped away. Except for a tinge of something foreign about the vowels he could have been educated at an English boarding school.

'You could always speak English,' I blurted.

'Yes, I have a gift for languages. I am also tolerably capable in French and am a student of Farsi – no easy tongue to master, by the way.'

I studied Ahmed's face. The high cheekbones, the doe eyes, the silky curtain that fell over his brow. How could we have ever believed he was a son of the soil – accustomed to scratching the earth for his living? Those soft hands had been nowhere near a plough.

'You're no more of a peasant than I am.'

'Certainly no one could accuse you of being a peasant. Your manners, as Miss Minchin will agree, are far too refined.'

'How dare you laugh at me!' Suddenly I was furious, my hurt feelings boiling over into rage. 'You – you traitor!'

'What's your game anyway?' Waldo cut in roughly. 'You after treasure?'

Ahmed tensed, becoming very still.

'So, now we find you are not a farmer. You weren't

even a stowaway on the *Maharani*, were you? How could we ever have thought that was possible? I mean how would you have survived for weeks in the hold without food or water? Not to mention the toilet. What were we thinking?'

'I am amazed it took you so long, Kit.'

'Miss Salter to you.'

'I apologise. Miss Salter.'

'Let's see, what other lies have you told us? I suppose the story of the scarab's curse was bunkum too.'

'I may have used a little dramatic licence, but in essence –'

'And your sick father,' I cut Ahmed off. 'I suppose that was a lie too, something you made up to pull at our heartstrings?'

'No! Believe me. My father had a heart attack when he heard of the theft of the mummy of Ptah Hotep. He has not spoken nor moved since that day. At this moment he is in a coma, more in the world of the dead than in the living.'

'You're lying,' I muttered.

'Poor Father,' he said looking down at the floor. 'He had already lost my brother – my older brother – Khalil. He died in a hunting accident when I was just ten years old. Khalil was always Father's golden boy, brave, generous, reckless. His death broke half father's heart. What

185

was left was destroyed by the theft of the scarab.'

'I'm not interested in your excuses,' I snapped.

But Ahmed continued, as if he was talking to himself: 'You see, Father blamed himself. He thought the theft of the scarab was all his fault. He is a proud man and –'

'Enough!' I cut him off. He sounded so sincere. But how could I really tell? Ahmed could be the finest actor I'd ever met. 'Why did you do this to us?' I asked. The anger was draining away leaving me wretched. 'We took you in, fed you, clothed you. Waldo fought a duel over this whole business. I thought you were our friend.'

Ahmed hung his head.

'Why treat us like *this*?'

'I am sorry. Really, believe me, I am sorry. You've been kind. I too, feel true friendship for you.'

'If this is how you treat your friends, thank goodness I'm not your enemy.'

'I will tell you the truth now. The whole truth.'

'We're listening,' I said.

'My father is a doctor, a learned man, who also happens to be the headman of our tribe. We live in a village near the ruins of the Pharaoh's old capital, Memphis. But we are no village idiots. Memphis is not far from Cairo, we travel, I go to school.'

'It is true that my father's brother lives in Cairo and that he has a wastrel son. This son Ali was employed by your aunt Hilda. Well, to cut a long story short he is a bad fellow, a real idle layabout. He looted the secret rock tomb of Ptah Hotep, after my father was indiscreet enough to reveal its hidden location. His gang of robbers got away with the sage's mummy and other wonderful relics. But these riches are as nothing compared with the treasures still hidden.'

'Finally,' breathed Waldo. 'We're getting to the point.'

Ahmed ignored the interruption 'You know about the scarab?'

'Of course.'

'This beetle is the charm that Ptah Hotep wore next to his heart, buried deep under layers of linen wrappings. It has lain undisturbed for thousands of years – time immemorial.'

'I thought we asked you to get to the point!'

'I am, Kit – Miss Salter, I am. My family contains many learned scholars. You see, we are Berbers. We are descended from the great Pharaohs. Their ancient blood lives on in our veins. It was my great-grandfather who entrusted my father with the scarab's secret. It contains the clue to buried treasure.'

'So this scarab isn't just your villagers' lucky charm?' I asked.

'Far from it,' he replied. 'It is a kind of map. If you can read it, it will take you to treasure. This secret is known only to a few Egyptian scholars – somehow the Baker Brothers must have learnt about it!'

'What treasure?' I asked.

'I do not know, except that it is meant to be fabulous.'

'You want it, don't you?' I said. 'You're as bad as the Bakers yourself.'

'NO!'

In his agitation Ahmed jumped right out of his chair and began to pace the room. 'You've got it all wrong. You must have seen what your fellow "explorers" and "Egyptologists" have done to our ancient heritage. They have pillaged priceless mastabas, wrecked pyramids. You have heard of "The Great Belzoni"? The circus strong-man?'

I nodded.

'When he found a beautiful wall covered in hiero-glyphics in Cairo's Valley of the Kings he smashed his way through it with a battering ram.'

'But he was an Italian. An English gentleman would not –'

'Please do not be so naive. The greatest robber in the whole game is Colonel Henry Vyse,' Ahmed inter-rupted. 'A few years ago he bored a hole in the Great Sphinx and when his boring rods got stuck, blew them free with dynamite. The Great Sphinx at Giza, the great-est statue in the world! Your explorers are no more than burglars! Vandals!'

'Egyptians have raided the pyramids too,' I protested, remembering my father's words on the subject. 'Hundreds of years ago the Arab rulers of Egypt, so my father told me, ransacked the pyramids for limestone to build Cairo.'

'What is England's oldest monument?' Ahmed changed the subject.

'Stonehenge?'

'How would you feel if a party of Egyptian explorers descended on Stonehenge and carted all the stones off to display in a museum in Cairo? How would you feel if they told you it was to keep them safe?'

I was silent.

'We Berbers are all that is left of the ancient Egyptians,' Ahmed raced on. 'My family feels it is our duty to protect our heritage. The treasures must remain buried. My father had his heart attack because he felt he had let his people down. He was shamed, Kit, shamed to his very soul. That is why he now lies in a coma, lost to his family and his people. I have to save the scarab and keep Ptah Hotep's treasure safe. It is the only way to help my father.'

'How do you expect us to believe you?' I asked softly. 'I mean you've lied about who you are. Now you're lying about this.'

'Kit, Waldo, I had to lie. How can I explain this to you? Egyptians are a proud people, we have a noble history stretching back to the times of the Pharaohs. Times – with no disrespect – when you in England were scarcely more than savages. But now we are weak and your empire with its boats and guns controls us. How would you have reacted if a proud Egyptian stranger stood before you and told you the tale you've learned today. You'd have mistrusted me. So I played on your pity. You took me in as a waif and stray and for that I am grateful!'

'How did you come to be in the box of the mummy anyway?' Waldo asked.

'Bad luck.' Ahmed shrugged. 'Truth to tell I ran away from home, after my father's heart attack, determined to find the scarab and restore his health. As you know, he was in a coma and in no position to stop me. I took a passage on the *Maharani*, following your aunt, Kit, and the mummy. At the stroke of midnight, on the last night of the voyage, I sneaked down to the hold in my nightshirt. I let myself in and was searching among the boxes for the one containing Ptah Hotep's mummy. Suddenly two sailors appeared. I was trapped. I climbed quietly into a large packing case; by an awful stroke of fate it was the very case containing Ptah Hotep's closed sarcophagus. I was caught like a rat, helpless, in a case which contained the very scarab I sought. A little later the sailors moved the packing case into another hold. I remember the sound as they turned the key. It was so final, so brutal. I was locked in, half out of my wits with fright.'

'There was nothing witless about the way you played us,' I said. I remembered Ahmed as we'd first met him, hungry, dirty, tangle-haired. In fact Ahmed's chrysalis to butterfly transformation had all happened so effortlessly we'd scarcely noticed. I still thought of him as the waif, unable to speak English, when he was anything but.

Which just goes to show how unobservant I am! You, I am sure, would do better. You would put your prejudices to one side and see more things more clearly. However, I must confess myself sadly blind. Still, lamenting my shortcomings was pointless. It would not help us solve the problem of what to do about Ahmed.

I stood up, looking clear into Ahmed's eyes: 'How can we ever trust you again?'

Ahmed slumped back in his chair. Silence hung over the room. I tried to think how we should act, but I felt hopelessly confused. Should we give Ahmed up to my aunt? Tell her about the scarab and the Baker Brothers' theft?

'There *may* be a way to put Ahmed to the test,' said Waldo.

❧ Chapter Twenty-one ❧

'This?' I whispered to Waldo, rolling my eyes in mock horror as I looked at the collection of eccentrics and lunatics around the table. '*This* is your big idea?'

'Shush, Kit,' he hissed. 'Don't be so prejudiced.'

I couldn't believe I had agreed to visit a seance at Waldo's mother's medium, in the hope that 'spirits' would put Ahmed to the test. Waldo was planning to ask Mrs Guppy to contact the other world. 'Spirit messengers' would let us know if Ahmed was telling the truth. Frankly, I was sceptical. I had never believed in mediums and all that mumbo jumbo. Yet any hope was better than none and Waldo had argued fiercely that we should give it a try. The scarab was slipping out of our reach. We desperately needed a breakthrough.

'Are you brave of heart?' Mrs Guppy voice's was a mere caressing murmur. 'Only the strongest souls should join me on my quest to contact the spirits. We shall travel beyond life. We shall meet spirits of loved ones and the ghosts of those unhappy souls who have not found peace. We shall commune with angels and fend off demons . . . '

The medium droned on, her voice hypnotic, soothing as the murmur of waves. It was too hot in her stuffy parlour. My eyes drooped, my body felt strangely light. Wake Up! I told myself fiercely. I could not afford to doze off, not now when I needed to be especially alert.

I glanced over at Ahmed, who was sitting next to Rachel. Was it my imagination that made him look particularly nervous? All my friends were here, except Isaac who recently had been slipping off by himself. On secret business of his own. Apart from us, there were five others round Mrs Guppy's ebony table; all of them tense and excited. Mrs Guppy, whose chair was higher than ours, towered over us with the air of a queen holding court. With her puffy face she looked like a dumpling in a curly wig. Only her eyes were unusual: periwinkle-blue and oddly transparent. I felt as if I was peering through a stained glass window to another world.

Waldo was very grave about the whole process, but looking around the table at the 'seekers after truth', I was unimpressed. Spiritualists were a very rum lot. There was a gent in a shabby morning coat, whose face was almost hidden by his whiskers. An enormously fat widow in mourning, her face hidden by a black veil. An unkempt captain of the merchant navy. Finally there was Mr Guppy, an insignificant-looking little man about whom I can tell you nothing – for he made no impression on me at all.

Something about these 'seekers' struck me as odd. I couldn't quite put my finger on it, but they were not right; there was something strange, almost sinister about them. All my nerves were jangling, warning me not to relax, not to give in to the soothing atmosphere of the seance. There was menace lurking around this table, I could feel it. What I couldn't tell was what form the danger would take.

'The lamp, dear,' Mrs Guppy reminded her husband. The lights were extinguished and a dreary half-twilight descended on the room.

'Let us cleanse our hearts of all impure elements,' intoned Mrs Guppy. 'The Lord's Prayer, my dear Mr Guppy, if you please.'

Mr Guppy chanted the Lord's Prayer and we all joined in. As our prayers continued a musky scent drifted through the air and a plangent wailing began. This startled me till I realised Mr Guppy was strumming on a guitar. On the table in front us were arrayed a variety of instruments including a violin, a banjo and a French horn.

'Join hands, let the healing energy flow through you.

Ishtar, Sahara, Gabriel . . . we implore your presence,' Mrs Guppy droned.

I linked hands with Ahmed on one side and the fat lady on the other. Her hand lay in my own like a hundredweight of ham. She hadn't observed mourning totally, for her fingernails were painted scarlet.

'I can feel them flowing through my limbs, igniting my nerves with their passions. The spirits are awake. They will visit us this day.'

On my left the widow gave a gasp of excitement. Before my very eyes the banjo, the violin and the horn rose in the air where they proceeded to strum and blast all at the same time. The widow's hand was trembling violently in my own. The banjo was so close to me I could stretch out and touch it. Then it levitated, higher, higher, its strings a-quiver.

I felt a thrill of awe.

Bang. All the instruments clattered to earth at the same time, falling with heavy thuds on the lace tablecloth and Turkey carpet. The din was silenced at a stroke, leaving our nerves jangling.

A ghostly apparition was floating out of the centre of the table. A silvery thumb, fingers splayed. A wonderful apparition, a spirit hand. Across the table Rachel was wide-eyed with wonder.

I had a sudden, wild impulse. I let go of my partner's

fingers and reached out for the spirit hand, intending to grab it. In doing so my feet banged against something under the table and the hand fell to the ground. It was all so dark and blurred I couldn't be sure, but I *thought* I saw a stick poking through a hole in the table, which rapidly closed up. A moment later the hand had vanished.

'We have a non-believer in the room.' Mrs Guppy leapt up, majestic in her rage. 'Who dares assault the sanctity of the seance?'

I had failed to catch the spirit hand, but in my clumsiness I had knocked over a jug of water. Liquid sloshed over the polished table, collecting in a little pool in the centre.

'Kit!' Waldo hissed, while all the others turned reproachful eyes on me.

'I'm sorry!' I muttered. I felt foolish and ashamed.

'You have no right to interrupt the seance; you'd never dare behave like this in church!' he fumed.

Mrs Guppy collapsed back into her chair, as if utterly exhausted. Her husband was fluttering around her. Waves of hostility were directed at me. Even Rachel was angry.

'The seance is at an end,' Mr Guppy announced.

Immediately everyone began to clamour, the whiskered man protesting he had paid dearly for a spirit communication and he wasn't going to have it ruined by some chit of a girl.

'Take no notice of Kit,' Waldo declared. 'She never could control herself.'

'The spirits have been insulted,' Mrs Guppy replied. 'They will not return this day.'

'Fine by me.' I pushed away my chair and stood up, glaring at Waldo. 'We're leaving.'

But none of my friends rose to support me.

Turning, I noticed Ahmed. He was taking no notice of the commotion but was instead staring, with an awed expression, at the pool of spilt water on the table. The puddle which had collected after the jug overturned. Puzzled, I followed his gaze. What was so fascinating? The water was just water. Silvery, a faint sheen of dust on its surface. I looked again. Then I saw.

Bubbling in the surface of the liquid was the impression of a man's face. Eyes, lips, nose, a hint of a whitish hair. Faint, but no mirage. Something was in that puddle. Angel or spirit. This was something real, not flesh and blood, but a thing that existed nevertheless.

'Father!' Ahmed croaked.

All around the room heads turned and a profound silence fell on the room. Ahmed reached out as if to touch the surface of the water, to stroke his father's face. The movement of air made the thing ripple, then it was still once more.

A careworn face, more dead than alive. I could see Ahmed in the fine, large eyes, the sculpture of the man's bones. With a difference, though. There was something hollow about this man. The image moved further from us, as if we were travelling away and there it was, a human skeleton lying on a simple wooden bed.

'Father. Forgive me.'

The image flickered and vanished and now something else appeared, a shining youth, bare foot. He looked like Ahmed, except older and somehow golden. He had the honey colour of desert sand dunes and there were yellow glints in his eyes. He smiled at us, merry, almost mocking. What was this? Were we all hypnotised? Perhaps we were all sunk in the same strange dream. Ahmed had jumped up and now he blurted a single, strangled word.

'Khalil!'

'You never thought you'd see *me* again.'

'How, brother?'

The boy Khalil shrugged, or at least I think that was what it was, for his image rippled and then reformed.

'I come about Father,' we heard the spirit say. At least we think that was what we heard. 'You must go home to him.'

'The scarab. I must find the scarab,' Ahmed pleaded.

'Gone, my little brother. You were never the wanderer. It was I who should have sailed the world. Your place, Ahmed, is at home.'

'I must find the scarab to help father. The scarab will bless us again and the treasure will be saved.'

'Come home. Father's time is short.'

A low moan came from across the table. Mrs Guppy was rigid, her face drawn with shock. She looked terrified. Suddenly I realised why. I would wager this was the first true spirit ever to have graced her parlour.

Ahmed's voice choked in his throat as the water flickered and fell still. It was just a puddle again. His brother – a ghostly messenger from twilight space between life and death – had gone.

'You *see*,' he turned to me and his eyes were full of tears. 'You see the truth now.'

'Oh, Ahmed,' I began, but I was cut off by a loud thump on the table.

'THAT'S ENOUGH!' a voice rang out. The fat lady had risen from her chair, a commanding figure in her black garments. The veil had fallen from her face. The drooping widow was gone. In her place was a harpy with cruel eyes, her mouth a slash of scarlet.

'You've had yourselves some fun and games. Time to get down to business,' she spat.

In her hand Velvet Nell held a pistol, pointed straight at my chest.

✎ Chapter Twenty-two ✎

'We bin patient as sheep,' said the whiskered man. 'Now it's time to turn tiger.'

With a lazy movement he tore off his moustache, revealing the insignificant mouth and weak chin of Bender Barney. He too had a gun, this one trained on Waldo.

I looked around the table: naval man, fat lady, whiskers. Not harmless spiritualists at all, but ruthless members of the Velvet Mob. I knew the so-called spiritualists seemed familiar, I had sensed danger. But I'd been fooled by the atmosphere of the seance. I had thought that the menace would be of the other-worldly kind. The thugs, all-too-human, surrounded us, each one bearing a gun. Rachel's scream echoed through the parlour. Mrs Guppy was so bewildered her mouth was opening and closing like goldfish.

'You cover the Egyptian,' Barney ordered the naval man. 'I've a history with this lad.' He grabbed Waldo by the ear and shoved him out of the room in front of him.

I followed, Velvet Nell's gun digging into my back.

'Thank you for your little show, Mrs Guppy,' Velvet Nell turned at the top of the stairs. 'I've a good mind to mention you to the management at the Alhambra. You could do a nice little turn there, after the performin' monkey.'

Mrs Guppy's doughy face crumpled. As for her husband, he had managed to melt into thin air.

The three thugs shepherded us down the stairs, covering us with their pistols every inch of the way. My breath was ragged, heart thump, thump, thumping. Maybe we could do something in the small space of the stairs. If I bumped into Waldo, who was in front of me, and he fell against the thug leading the way – then if Ahmed tripped up the naval man . . .

'None of your tricks now,' Velvet Nell snapped, as if she could read my mind. 'Try any fancy moves and I'll put one through your head.'

We tumbled out into the smog of Kensington High Street. A cab was waiting, the driver smoking a gasper. He winked at the mob, threw it away and picked up the reins. Barney opened the door and gave Waldo another push.

'In yer get,' he snapped.

'Not so fast, Barney,' Velvet Nell commanded.

'Wot?'

'I said let's teach 'em a lesson, we don't need to drag along the whole bleeding pack of 'em.'

'I want the boy.'

'Sorry. Not today.'

Barney glowered, but a glance from the woman squashed him flatter than a rat under the wheels of an omnibus. Clearly it was Nell who gave the orders. She walked by, inspecting us closely, then stopped by Rachel.

'We'll take her,' she said, stroking Rachel's ringlets with the nozzle of her gun, an elegant weapon with a mother-of-pearl handle. 'She won't be half as much trouble. Come along, dear.' Her fingers closed around Rachel's arm and she turned to us. 'Now you run along, children, and keep out of trouble. I warn you, one squeak out of you, your pretty little friend gets it. She wouldn't look half so nice with a bullet in her skull.'

'Take me instead,' I blurted.

'You're a troublemaker. I can tell these things straight off.'

'Please.'

'I made meself quite clear. You keep your noses out of other people's business and your friend here will be unharmed. One step out of line and she's coffin filler. Clear?'

Miserably, I nodded.

Rachel had not uttered a word. Her face was pale and she moved like a sleepwalker as Barney took over from Nell and shoved her roughly into the cab. Nell kept us covered with her pistol, she was the last to climb in. Once all the thugs were inside with their captive she looked out and waved at us gaily. Then she yelled a command to the driver and the horses started up, clipping through the traffic at a breakneck speed.

'No!' I shouted, the word ringing out of me like a pistol shot

It was too late. The traffic surged, swallowing up the cab and Rachel with it.

❧ Chapter Twenty-three ❧

'Wait,' Ahmed called after the thugs. 'I can help you. I'll do anything you ask. I will –' he stopped mid-sentence, his words hanging broken in the air. 'This is all my fault.'

'No. I'm to blame.' Waldo said. 'If I hadn't had that stupid idea about going to the seance.'

'What's wrong with you?' I cut in. 'What does it matter whose fault this is? We should be halfway to Belgravia or the East End or I don't know, Cornwall by now. Quick. Stop a cab. I bet they're going to the Bakers' castle in Cornwall.'

'Forget Cornwall!' a voice rang out.

A cab had drawn up, a skinny grime-spattered figure leaning out of the door.

'Hop in,' the dirty shape yelped.

Waldo gaped at the person, unsure whether it was another kidnapper or merely an odd stranger. 'Where have you been, Isaac?' I said as I ushered us all into the cab. It was my friend, under several layers of what looked like Thames mud. Once we were all in, Isaac was just about to start talking when I shushed him. Instead I bellowed to the driver.

'Follow that cab!'

'What cab?' The man asked, looking where I was pointing. 'Any particular cab in mind?'

The road was choked with cabs, of all shapes and sizes.

'It doesn't matter. That direction. And get a move on.'

'Follow that cab the little lady says, as if I'm a bloomin' magician.'

Grumbling, the cabby whipped his horses and we rumbled off, clattering past the rest of the traffic. Past the Royal Albert Hall and towards the snaking blue thread of the Serpentine. Here the traffic suddenly thinned out and there hoved into view the mob's cab, going at a fantastic pace.

As the horses galloped I explained Rachel's kidnapping to Isaac, in a few words. The hardest words I have ever had to say. He went very quiet. The cab lurched after the gangsters and Waldo hung out of the door, urging the driver to push the horses ever harder.

Where were we going? The mob had turned past Hyde Park and gone down towards the river. Then along the Thames, passing the Strand and going east.

'The East End,' I said. 'The Velvet Mob must have

some sort of hide-out there.'

'You're wrong,' Isaac said, coming out of his reverie. His tongue tripping in his hurry, he started to tell us about one of his new inventions, a device he'd named a 'telesphere'. It seemed that a telesphere was a sort of extendable ear that our brilliant friend had invented, a kind of bell-shaped receiver linked to a device Isaac carried. It sounded improbable, mad! I could see Waldo and Ahmed were sceptical from the looks they gave me. Don't ask me how it worked for I haven't a clue. I freely admit that I only understand a quarter of what goes on in Isaac's head. Anyway, the telesphere was the 'secret' Isaac had been so quiet about over the last few days. When we lost him at the Baker Brothers' he had, in fact, been planting a telesphere in their study. For the last few days he had skulked around their house, listening for useful information. To no avail, mostly. It seemed the Baker Brothers kept a most monastic silence. Besides, though Isaac was a little cagey about this, his device didn't *always* work – and what he did hear tended to be a little muffled.

Two hours ago though, Isaac, our hero, had finally come up trumps. He had overheard the secretary and the servants discussing their master's travelling plans. Cook was complaining that she was expected to provide a feast for the Bakers to take on the *Morning Star* – with only a few hours' notice. The secretary, meanwhile, called cook a 'lazy pudding' and sniffed that a bit of work would do her good.

The meaning of the exchange was startling.

The two brothers were not going to their Cornish castle after all. They were setting sail for Cairo aboard the *Morning Star,* a P & O steamer. They were leaving from West India Dock that very afternoon. Reluctant to trust their minions with such a fabulous haul they were going after the Pharaoh's treasure themselves.

'You think they're taking Rachel to Egypt?' Ahmed gasped.

'It looks that way,' Isaac said. In front of us, almost hidden behind a hansom carriage was the mob's black and gold vehicle. 'They are already three-quarters of the way to West India docks.'

'We have to stop them,' I said. 'Even if it means going all the way to Egypt.'

The Docks. Stench, clanging and the hubbub of a thousand different tongues pressed upon us. The entire world had descended upon this corner of London. Africans in brilliant robes, Chinamen running hither and thither. Indians, Arabs, Lascars, Italians. Bales of cinnamon and ginger, tea and coffee pouring into giant warehouses. It was dangerous to stand still for more than a second for a thundering trolley would send you reeling. Worst of all, you might get in the way of one of the enormous swinging winches, used for unloading pallets from ships.

We'd seen the empty cab at the entrance to the docks, but in among all the chaos we had completely lost Rachel and her kidnappers.

Over in one corner of the docks was a bedraggled queue: men, women and children waiting. Even the tots were bowed down by bags, bundles wrapped in sacking, pots and pans. I was wondering who these people were, when I suddenly understood. They were emigrants, preparing to leave Europe behind and set sail for the new world. Baruch and Sarah might well be in that queue, or one like it.

'This is hopeless,' I moaned. 'It's like bedlam here. What are we going to do?'

'Ask at the P & O passenger office,' Isaac said. 'Find out when the *Morning Star* departs for Egypt.'

'No need,' Waldo murmured.

'You have any better ideas?' I snapped.

'It's a little too late for that!' He was pointing at something, an object in the crowded mouth of the docks.

My eyes followed Waldo's finger. Pulling away from us was a splendid steamship. For a moment I didn't see

the lettering, stretching proud along her sides. Then I
took it in.

The Morning Star

'The *Morning Star*'s leaving,' I said stupidly.

The ship was racing out of the docks, creating a broad
wash as it pounded past merchant vessels and river tugs.
Modern and fast and splendid. The finest steamer
money could buy. We could make out two figures on the
deck. One was the potato shape of Bender Barney
Beside him, slim and dark, hung Rachel. Even from port
I could tell she was listless, in the way she drooped over
the ship's rails.

From beside me came a wild howl. It was Ahmed. He
pulled off his coat, clearly he meant to leap into the
Thames.

'Ahmed!' I screamed, trying to grab him.

'I'm a good swimmer,' he yelled back, pushing me
away. 'It's the only way to save Rachel now!'

He gave an almighty jump and landed in the Thames,
thick with the contents of London's sewers. Oily green
liquid bubbled and boiled around his neck as he swam
with strong strokes towards the *Morning Star*.

'Don't be a bloody fool,' yelled Waldo.

Ahmed had miscalculated. The water in the Thames

was foul, too heavy to swim in. At every stroke some bit of debris held him back and we could see his shoulders sinking under the effort. Meanwhile, the steamer was chugging away to the open seas, far too fast for Ahmed to catch. The thugs on deck turned and walked off as we watched.

I looked around and found a rope. With all my strength I hurled it in and Ahmed, thank goodness, caught hold of one end of it. The others assisted me, using all our strength we pulled Ahmed out. Finally he was up on the dock, soaked through and stinking of raw sewage. Worse than the smell though, was the despair on his face.

'That's it then,' I said, watching the *Morning Star* recede into the distance, chugging past all the other boats and ships in the port. Ahmed, wet and stinking, was shivering beside me. I would have to find him some clean clothes. We would have to try and find a passage to Egypt. It wouldn't be easy though, I knew that. Steamship tickets were hard to find. Rachel, meanwhile, sailed away from us.

'Hold on a minute.' Isaac was gazing at something coughing into port. 'NEVER GIVE UP! It was you, Kit, who taught me that.'

'Not now, Isaac!'

'Good Lord, what's that?' Waldo cut in. He was staring at the same object as Isaac, out among the flotilla of boats.

I followed his gaze. Steaming into harbour was a vessel one could hardly describe as a ship. More of an old tin tub really, with two rusty-looking funnels belching foul smoke. *Poonah* was written on the side of boat, in cracked green paint.

'That, my friend,' said Isaac with a smile, 'is the rescue party.'

I scanned the boat. There on the fore-deck was a sight I had never expected to see in this life or any other. Standing side by side, grinning away, the unlikely pair of Aunt Hilda and Gaston Champlon.

'Explain!' I snapped, turning to Isaac. 'What on earth is going on?'

Part Three

Each of these maxims should be handed down so they
never disappear from this land.
Maxim 38, *The Wisdom of Ptah Hotep*

∾ Chapter Twenty-four ∾

'I admit it. Sometimes I jump to conclusions.'

'Sometimes, Aunt Hilda?' I asked.

'Occasionally, then.'

'I was going to say usually. Take the case of the mummy. You had absolutely *no evidence* for stomping around town blaming poor Monsieur Champlon for the theft.'

'Call it gut feeling.'

'Your gut was wrong, Auntie. That's the whole point. You should stop listening to your gut and start listening to your brain.'

Normally I wouldn't have dared talk to her like this, but Aunt Hilda was being so contrite I just couldn't resist. It was five days after the terrible scenes at West India Docks and we were aboard the *Poonah*, chasing the villains on the *Morning Star* through the high seas.

'It is ze ledees' right to be wrong,' interrupted Champlon, who had joined me and my aunt on our

215

stroll around the deck. He favoured us with a charming smile and offered his arm to Aunt Hilda, who took it grudgingly. 'Ledees are so emotional. I excuse them because ledees are not for ze t'inking. Zey are like ze soft rabbit.'

It is hard to imagine someone less like a soft rabbit than my aunt. She was about to snap at him, but I silenced her with a frown. She was on her very best behaviour these days, the sort of thing that counts as normal everyday manners from you and me. As you may imagine, this enforced courtesy wasn't easy for her. Isaac had worked a near miracle in bringing her round. It was my clever friend – and his telesphere – who had convinced both Aunt Hilda and Champlon that the Baker Brothers had stolen the mummy. It was Isaac's doing that we were here at all, aboard the *Poona* sailing to Egypt to rescue Rachel and the scarab. Isaac had well and truly saved the day.

'Anyway, madame,' Champlon continued. 'Ve must not fight each wiz ze other. Our enemy is ze Baker Brothers. 'Ow strange to think of them taking Ptah Hotep's mummy back to Egypt.'

I was not at all sure if the Baker Brothers were taking the mummy back to Egypt. Indeed I believed they would only bother with the scarab. But my aunt and Champlon had no idea of the scarab's existence, so I held my tongue.

'We must rescue Ptah Hotep from these villains,' Champlon continued.

'And of course, young Rebecca,' Aunt Hilda said as an afterthought.

'Her name is Rachel,' I put in stoutly.

'Yes. Rachel,' my aunt replied. 'That's what I said.'

In a frenzy of preparations for our dash to Egypt, Aunt Hilda had hired the *Poonah* complete with captain and crew. The battered old steamer was the best she could find in a hurry. And off we sped.

Well, that was the idea.

In fact, the *Poonah* was marooned in the waters of the Mediterranean. It was like being stuck in a giant bath tub. The wind was taking us nowhere fast, but the doughty little steamer persevered, its gallant engines coughing on. I had reason to be grateful to the *Poonah*. Though it looked like a piece of scrap metal, it was a fighter, as determined as the rest of us to catch our prey. Still, we had seen nothing resembling the *Morning Star* for days. Then a few minutes before, Ahmed, who spent hours hanging over the deck rails, had seen a white and red blur on the horizon sailing in the direction of Alexandria. You can guess what happened next. Aunt Hilda was all for firing on the ship, though we had just one rusty old cannon, whose balls would have plopped harmlessly into the sea.

Anyway, the whole debate soon became irrelevant because the *Morning Star* – if indeed it was our enemy's ship – disappeared again over the horizon.

'We're never going to catch them,' I said, turning away from the sea.

It was hard not to feel despondent. Rachel was imprisoned somewhere in a fast modern steamship. Try as we might, we couldn't compete. True, our boat had red and black port and starboard funnels, which belched out more smoke than a bonfire, while the paddle wheels churned furiously. Though I knew it was ungrateful I felt a stab of anger towards the *Poonah*. All that energy with so little result. We were the tortoise of ocean-going steamers. How could we ever rescue our friend? How would we ever seize back the scarab?

'Do not worry,' Ahmed said. 'I'll have a few tricks up my sleeve when we reach Egypt.'

'What do you have in mind?'

'I have friends,' Ahmed murmured and to my frustration would say no more.

It was too much. The *Poonah* had been on the seas for days; sailing from West India docks in London around Italy then on to Athens, where we refuelled for the trip across the Mediterranean to Alexandria in Egypt. Sometimes I felt we were on a fool's errand. Even if we had been able to catch up with the *Morning Star* how could we – with our half-dozen crew members – take on the Velvet Mob?

'You may say we'll have the upper hand in Egypt,' I muttered gloomily. 'But they've beaten us every time so far.'

Ahmed merely shrugged, then stalked away. Sullen, I hung over the rail and stared at the sea. Not that there was anything to look at, unless you like watching seagulls. Water, waves, crests of foam and spray around the paddle-wheel. I could never be a sailor. The sight of so much emptiness would drive me to distraction. Rachel would have coped better with seafaring life. She had the patience to endure. Though it was strange, with Rachel gone, I found myself far more cautious than usual. It was almost as if I was listening to an echo of my friend's voice inside my own head. An echo that stilled my most reckless thoughts.

'Lunchtime yet?' Isaac emerged from his cabin, blinking.

'I'm famished. Let's ask the captain,' I replied.

The captain and first mate were in the pilot house, a rickety wooden shed on the top deck. Their voices were raised in loud argument, but when I opened the door it stopped abruptly.

'I was wondering what happened to lunch?' I said. 'It is nearly two o' clock.'

'Better ask Cook,' the captain replied with a sharp glance at the first mate, a man called Simpson who wandered around the boat like gloom personified. 'Simpson. Find out what's happened to lunch.'

'Aye, aye, sir,' Simpson said, managing to make even those simple words sombre.

The captain and Isaac began a technical discussion about the boiler. Isaac had an idea for cutting down on fuel use which truth to tell I didn't understand, so I decided to go down into the galley and see how lunch was coming on. The kitchen was a low wooden room beneath the quarter-deck. A selection of cheap tin pots and pans hung from beams. It was poorly lit and everything was coated with a layer of soot from the ancient stove. Cook's white apron and hat loomed out of the murk. He was bending over the stove stirring something – which to be honest did not smell too promising.

'Hello,' I asked the man's back. 'What's for luncheon?'

Cook turned round. With a shock I saw Simpson's mournful face peering out from under the hat: ''Ash. Always 'ash round 'ere.'

'Where's Cook?'

'You're looking at 'im.'

'Pardon?' I spluttered.

'I'm the bleedin' cook. This ain't the *Mornin' Star*, you know. We ain't got a crew of thousands toiling away down here to dish up dainties for yer grub.'

'How . . . nice,' I said, lamely. 'How long will it be?'

'Five minutes. Just got to get the hash warmed up.'

I stared at the pot a moment; something brown and lumpy coated in lashings of brown gloop lurked in the depths.

'I'll go and ring the lunch bell.'

When I reached the upper deck to round everyone up for lunch, I heard several loud bangs. Waldo was starboard, leaning over the side of the railings, firing his duelling pistol at an imaginary target out at sea.

'Isn't it time you hung up your pistols, Waldo?'

'Not till I can hit a shark at half a furlong,' he replied, sending another bullet scudding into the waves.

'Oh for goodness' sake, you'd better ask Champlon if you want shark for luncheon.'

'Why don't you ever have faith in me?' he snapped, glaring at me.

While Waldo and I were bickering, Gaston Champlon and Aunt Hilda rounded the deck, apparently in perfect harmony. The pair of explorers might have patched up their differences but Waldo still remained sulky around the Frenchman. Not that Champlon noticed. He spied Waldo's gun and a smile wreathed his face.

'I will show you 'ow,' he said, trying to wrest the pistol from Waldo's hands. 'You are 'olding 'er wrong. A

221

pistol is like a lady. You woo 'er, win 'er, handle 'er in ze graceful manner.'

Waldo snarled and I placed myself between them to stop a fight.

'Lunchtime,' I reminded them. 'Cook's whipped up something special.'

'Special?' Aunt Hilda burst out, throwing down her spoon in disgust. 'I expect the mongrel dogs prowling outside my house would turn their noses up at this.'

We were in the dining room, a cabin that in its heyday must have been rather elegant. Now the chandelier was missing most of its crystal drops and the mahogany table was battered. Like the rest of the boat the room needed a good lick of paint. Isaac, who was so absent-minded he could eat boiled earwigs without turning a hair, was guzzling the food, but the rest of us were pushing the stuff around our plates.

'We've got to economise on the food,' said Isaac, who took a great interest in the practicalities of the voyage. 'We can't risk running out of grub before we reach Alexandria.'

'I've never lived on such mush,' Aunt Hilda said. 'Even on my expedition to Tanganyika we had pemmican.'

'What on earth is pemmican?'

'Five ninths of pounded dry meat to four ninths of melted grease. Boiled up in some water with a little mashed yam it is perfectly nutritious. If my old explorer friends Burke and Wills had some pemmican in their foolish dash over Australia they wouldn't have starved to death. They should have come to me for advice, I'm always ready to help.'

'The hash has some vegetables in it today,' I said, though I wasn't sure the lumps under the brown gravy had any natural origin.

'It's worth it, for Rachel's sake,' Ahmed said and bravely gulped down a spoonful.

'No one could be more concerned for the safety of young Rebecca than I,' Aunt Hilda protested. No one bothered to correct her misnomer this time. It was impossible to shift an idea that had become lodged in her head. 'However, I do believe we are paying rather too heavy a price.'

'I agree with madame,' said Champlon. 'No ledee should 'ave to eat zis muck. And for a Frenchman from the land of haute cuisine it is insupportable.'

'You're grown men and women but you're acting like children! You couldn't care less about Rachel. All you're worried about is that stupid scarab!' Isaac burst out furiously. His face was all scrunched up and he looked as though he might burst into tears at any moment. I realised his show of calm over his sister was just a front. Inside a torrent had been building up.

'Scarab?' Monsieur Champlon looked alert as a moustached bloodhound on a new trail. 'What scarab?'

Silence fell on the room as Isaac flushed, realising his gaffe. It had been impressed on Isaac time and again that Champlon and Aunt Hilda must not be told of the scarab. A sudden gust of wind swept up a flurry of dust and set the broken chandelier tinkling.

'Goodness! This is very interesting.' My aunt turned to me, her face so alive with suspicion I already felt the lameness of any excuse I could come up with. When, oh, when would this interminable voyage come to an end? It seemed like some imp of discontent was abroad on the boat, making fools of us all.

'My dear Kit, what is this? You never mentioned a scarab!' Hilda continued. 'Are you keeping things from *me*?'

At that very moment a joyful cry sliced through the air:

'LAND AHOY! LAND AHOY!'

'Egypt!' I gasped, jumping to my feet.

The ship gave a mighty lurch as we all rushed on to deck for the first, thrilling glimpse of Africa. I had got away with it! Our secret was safe, for the sight of Egypt had made Aunt Hilda forget all about the scarab. And what a sight! The sea stretched in a dull greenish bowl ending in a line of froth and there on the horizon the markings of shore. Brown, flat, bare; the harshness relieved only by the thrusting spires of minarets. Egypt, the ancient land of the Pharaohs!

❧ Chapter Twenty-five ❧

'You're totally muddled, my boy. I always stay at Shepheard's when I am in Cairo,' my aunt barked at the receptionist. 'Good heavens, I'm doing you a favour. I'm told people travel to this hotel just for a chance of *glimpsing* me.'

'Gaston Champlon is also famous 'ere,' the Frenchman put in, unwilling to be outshone by my aunt.

'We are honoured to have your custom but at the moment we are fully booked,' the receptionist murmured. 'Please may I suggest the New Hotel?'

'That hovel? A place for tradesmen and spies. Remember, boy, you are speaking to *the* Hilda Salter.'

While my aunt and Champlon argued with the receptionist I turned away to the splendid lobby of Shepheard's Hotel; acres of marble resplendent with gleaming ebony panelling and date palms in massive pots. My aunt had informed me that it was the place to stay in Cairo. Here flitted waiters in the small bucket-shaped red hats the locals call tarbooshes, tiny braided jackets and puffy white trousers. There stalked missionaries off to convert the heathen, sweating in their starched white suits and palm-leaf hats. Was that man followed by porter weighed down with bags a collector in search of mummies or a invalid taking a cruise down the Nile for his health? Among the Westerners who thronged Shepheard's were Frenchmen, Americans and Greeks – surely spies, treasure-hunters and those who sought their fortune at the court of the Pasha?

Dozens of idlers lounged on the sun-soaked terraces outside Shepheard's watching life on Cairo's busiest boulevard. A street bustling with laden donkeys, Turkish carpet dealers, veiled women carrying water jugs on their heads, Bedouin tribesmen in billowing cream tunics. How can I give a feeling for the true wonder of Cairo? The domes of the pyramids rising in the desert-fringed distance. The sizzling kebabs on the street side stalls, the scent of spicy curries and sweet rosewater, the swelling, swaying mass of folk of all shades and manner of dress. It was strange and fascinating to me. How I wished we were free to wander awhile in the exotic streets; with their teetering fretwork upper-storeys, like vast bird cages on the point of collapse. Alas, we weren't here for sightseeing. Like a drumbeat in my head was Rachel, Rachel, Rachel.

I didn't care where we stayed. All that mattered was that we find my best friend. When I turned back to impress this on my aunt, the owner had been called, a deferential Swiss gentleman. He informed my aunt in soothing tones that he had been able to find a suite of rooms for her party. Typically she had won her battle! Soon after, bellboys arrived to take our luggage to our rooms – though I had just one small bag and protested I could manage myself. We were installed in rooms with a balcony overlooking the green oasis of the Ezbekiya Gardens opposite the hotel, one of the best suites in the hotel. I was weary and travel-stained. I freshened up with the jug of water on the marble washstand, then went to find Ahmed.

He was outside on the verandah, huddled with Isaac and Waldo. Tumblers of fresh lime juice stood on the table in front of them. It was so tangy it made the teeth at the back of my mouth sting. Just what I needed to slough off the dust of travel.

'So?' I asked Ahmed.

He looked very grave: 'I have some bad news, Kit.'

'Don't spare me.'

'I made enquiries and found a friendly bellboy. At least he became friendly after I paid him a few dinar. He told me there was a party of Europeans staying here. A couple of men, blond hair, very pale. They ate in their bedroom. Did not appear in the dining-room at all. With them was a party of a different type, not the usual customers at Shepheard's at all. The boy said they were rough. There was a beautiful woman with them. He went into raptures over her. Enormously fat, with the whitest skin and bluest eyes our bellboy had ever seen.'

I took a sip of lime water, choking a little as it went down to fast: 'Velvet Nell.'

'Kit, that isn't the worst of it though –' Ahmed broke off, as if scared to continue.

'Rachel,' I said.

'They had something with them. They brought it up the back stairs in a covered cage. Something they kept in a separate room. Our bellboy thought it must be a rare animal. He thought they were animal smugglers. Anyway he sneaked into the room. It was a young girl. A lovely girl, with her dark curls spread out over the pillow. She was asleep on the bed, fully clothed in her travelling dress. He was so surprised when he saw her close up that he stumbled and one of the glasses of water he was carrying on a tray fell over. It splashed on her face, Kit, but –'

'She didn't wake up,' Isaac said in a low voice.

'I'll kill them,' I said, so angry I could barely speak.

'At least she's alive,' Isaac murmured, more as if he was trying to convince himself than to me.

'They've drugged Rachel. I wouldn't have thought even the Velvet Mob could have behaved with such cruelty.'

'Probably some sort of sleeping draught,' Isaac said. 'My guess is that they gave it to her at the hotel to keep her quiet.'

Dark fears were gnawing at me. Rachel who wouldn't hurt anybody, the kindest, most truly good person I knew. How could anyone wish to harm her?

'Where are they?' I said.

'Wait, Kit.' Waldo put his hand on my arm. 'This party, they left yesterday morning. They're way ahead of us.'

'Let's not sit around chatting about it. We've got to go after them!'

'Where?' Waldo asked.

'What do you mean?'

'We do not know where they have gone,' Ahmed interrupted gently. 'They may have hired a dahabeeyah and gone down the Nile. They may have taken camels across the desert. We do not know where these people are headed.'

'They're probably going to Memphis. Isn't that where the scarab comes from?'

'It is not so simple, Kit,' Ahmed said patiently. 'They may have gone to my home town and of course I have my own reasons for going back fast but we do not know –'

'Your father!' I blurted overcome with a wave of remorse. My poor friend. Not only did he have Rachel to worry about, he must also be so worried about his dying father.

He ignored me: 'The most sensible plan is for me to ask around and see if anybody knows where they are headed. Meanwhile, Kit, I think you should take your aunt and Champlon and stock up on provisions for our journey.'

I wonder if you have ever shopped for provisions for a long desert journey? If you have you will know it is a tiring business. I had been looking forward to my first visit to Cairo's famous Khan Al Khalil bazaar: narrow, winding streets densely packed with the stalls of turbaned merchants selling everything from amber to sweetmeats to bubbling water-pipes called shishes. Four long hours later, spent trooping around after my aunt and Champlon as she haggled over the price of everything from saddles to sugar, I'd have been happy never to see another bazaar. The din was constant, the chaos and variety of goods startling. I was forced to acknowledge that without Aunt Hilda I'd have been at a loss. Would you, for example, know that you must take a small pair of forceps on a desert trek? If you do not and your horse becomes lame you will be stuck indeed, because there will be no way to remove the thorn. You could scorch to death.

After we had bought more provisions for our journey than I had thought possible we returned to the hotel, where Ahmed told us what he had learnt. After we had dressed for dinner – even in the East, apparently, such tedious English customs are observed – we all gathered in the restaurant. Aunt Hilda was wearing an evening dress of emerald velvet with a lace trim. A string of pearls nestled in her bosom. I had never observed such finery on her before and part of me wondered if she was hoping to attract Monsieur Champlon's attentions. Being the soul of gallantry, the Frenchman was most generous with his compliments:

'Blooming amid ze desert sands, ze fair rose of Cairo!'

'Nonsense,' Hilda mumbled, blushing. 'Order a bottle of claret if you please, monsieur. I'm absolutely parched.'

The restaurant at Shepheard's was a glorious sight; a cavern of a room held up with pillars, the walls richly ornamented with Arabic carvings. Through the vast space stretched many dozens of tables, topped by snowy linen and glittering crystal. The dresses of the women were no less brilliant. I have seldom seen such a profusion of diamonds, emeralds and rubies. I could fancy that the room was crowded with countesses and dukes;

the kings and queens of Europe could dine here. My steak and kidney pudding was excellent. A miracle that the hotel chefs could produce such fare from the bazaars of Cairo, though I suspected the steak was more horse than cow.

'Who are all these people?' I asked my aunt, looking around at the fashionable throng.

'Lightweights,' she snorted. 'Mere tourists for the most part. Egypt is most fashionable in Europe nowadays, which I suppose is partly my fault for writing such exciting books. Though I blame that pest of a man Thomas Cook more. Ever since he started his tours down the Nile there have been streams of riff-raff coming here for their health. They infest the place. Get in the way of serious Egyptologists.'

'Such a nuisance for you.'

'They should be banned. Hello! Who's over there?' My aunt had half-risen and was peering at a solitary diner in the corner of the room. He was an Egyptian-looking fellow, dressed in a cream suit. His black hair was smoothed down with grease. When my aunt pointed him out Ahmed stiffened and grabbed my arm, his fingers gripping too hard.

'I do believe it's my old friend Ali,' Aunt Hilda exclaimed. 'What a stroke of luck! Ali worked for me last time I was here. In fact he helped me find the mummy of Ptah Hotep.' She signalled to a passing waiter who glided over. 'Present the compliments of Hilda Salter to the gentleman in the corner. Ali whatsisname. Ask him to join us for a brandy.'

'Stop her,' Ahmed hissed in my ear. 'That's my cousin. He is a bad person.' The waiter had left and few minutes later the smooth young man stood by our table, a pleasant smile on his lips. He bowed to us all and then with an even broader grin, turned to Ahmed.

'My little cousin. Are you well, Ahmed?'

'Quite well,' my friend said, making it sound like a curse.

'It is indeed a pleasure to meet such good friends in these surroundings.'

Aunt Hilda was beaming. 'This settles it. Tomorrow we ride early to Memphis. Would you accompany us as guide and interpreter?'

'I can interpret for you,' Ahmed put in but Ali had already accepted the job offer. They were very alike, the cousins, doe-eyed and strong boned. Whereas Ahmed could be stiff and awkward, Ali was all silk and honey.

I retired soon after dinner, determined to be fresh for our early start. In the corridors outside our rooms Ahmed stopped us.

'I don't like this,' he hissed. 'Ali is rotten.'

'You're exaggerating,' Isaac said.

'Seems like a nice enough fellow,' said Waldo.

''Nice! My cousin would not know "nice" if you served it to him for dinner!' snapped Ahmed. 'He is bad. Please be careful. I think he is their spy.'

'Hold on, Ahmed,' Isaac said. 'He doesn't even know the Baker Brothers or the Velvet Mob. I know he pulled a pretty mean trick on your family but that –'

'I think we should listen to Ahmed,' I interrupted him. 'This is his homeland. He knows his cousin.'

'All I ask is be aware. Do not trust my filthy cousin. Do not tell him anything!'

I went to bed with Ahmed's words ringing in my ears. It was a chilly night, though that didn't stop the droning of mosquitoes. The little blood-suckers loved to feast on foreign flesh. Shepheard's Hotel, standing in the middle of large gardens, was particularly bad for the insects. I crawled under the mosquito net, extinguished my gas lamp and laid my head on the pillow.

One of my blessings is that I sleep extremely well. Tonight, however, I found it hard to drop off. It didn't help that there was a pack of wild dogs fighting some-where under my window. I'm sure English mongrels do not make such a nuisance of themselves. When I did finally fall asleep, I was plagued by strange dreams. I was travelling down the Nile, light as a bird skimming over the twinkling waters. My arms were sails, hovering this way and that. My feet touched the water but didn't get wet. Then slowly the river changed, and a low, tuneful melody started up. The Nile was no longer a thing of sparkling light and glory but an encircling net. It snaked around me in the darkness; oily, glistening, threatening to strangle me.

Panic bubbling inside me, I awoke with a start. That noise! With relief I realised it was only the muezzin, wailing from the top of his minaret, the call to prayer. This uncanny noise is a familiar sign here, a bit like the church bells ringing back home. God is great, the muezzin sang in his mournful heathen language. Everything was all right.

Or was it? As my eyes grew used to the gloom I saw something on top of my mosquito net. Bright eyes watched me. The thing glided down, making its way inexorably towards me. Dimly I saw glistening scales. A hood puffed up over its eyes, as it hissed. Someone had torn the net, leaving a hole for the snake to crawl through. I froze. Everything I'd ever heard about cobras flashed through my mind. If I was very careful, if I didn't provoke it, I would have a chance of getting away. Cobras only lashed out if they were scared, I tried to tell myself. All the time I was aware that if the cobra bit me, I could die.

❧ Chapter Twenty-six ❧

Mouth very dry, palms sweating, I slowly sat up in the bed. No sudden movements, I told myself. I inched back against the wall, keeping my eyes lowered. The snake was hissing to show how angry it was, a slow continuous noise, like escaping gas. I drew up my knees till they were under my chin. Most of me wanted to bolt, right then and there, but I knew that would be fatal. The snake would have struck, too quick and sure for me to have any chance. My only hope lay in keeping my head.

I levered my body out of the bed, as slow as I could manage. I was so close to the cobra I could have reached my hand out and stroked it. I'd read somewhere that if you touch the back of a cobra's neck, on the correct nerve, it goes limp and you can carry it like a length of rope. I was not so foolish as to believe I could manage this snake-charmer's trick.

I was out of the bed, away from the cobra's fangs. A clock chimed as I opened the door to my room. It was unlocked, though of course I had locked it before I retired to bed. Safely outside I let all my fright come pouring out and I screamed and screamed, like I never have before in my life. Down the corridors doors opened. Guests in nightcaps and gowns tumbled out of their rooms, cross and groggy. Among them were my friends. Ahmed quickly understood my story and a bell-boy, who had been asleep in the corridor, was despatched to find the gardener. Minutes later he returned with the man and we all followed him into my bedroom.

The cobra had curled up and gone to sleep in the middle of my bed as peacefully as a kitten. It gleamed against the white sheets; hard to believe now that I had been so scared of it. We watched as the gardener picked it up with a forked stick, holding it away from his body. Now we could see the splendid snake in its true light. It writhed and hissed furiously, spitting venom in a poison-ous spray. The gardener was cool as anything, he flicked it with his finger and suddenly it went all limp. The snake was unconscious.

'He will not hurt it. We Egyptians have worshipped snakes since the time of the Pharaohs. He will take it away. To the other side of Ezbekiya Gardens,' Ahmed explained. 'This man is very good with all wild things.'

'Why does everything happen to you, Kit?' Waldo

exclaimed, jealously. I was about to explode at him, to tell him it was actually horribly frightening to wake up with a great snake in one's mosquito net when Ahmed interrupted:

'It was my cousin, Ali. He put the snake in your mosquito net.'

'What?' I gaped at him. 'Why do you say that?'

'This bears all the marks of Ali. It is just his style. I tell you, Kit, I remember his sense of humour from when he came to stay at our house during the holidays. I am sure it was him. I know it in my bones.'

'My bedroom door was unlocked,' I said slowly. 'I'm absolutely sure I locked it before I went to bed. And my mosquito net. I remember now. Someone had torn it so there was a hole for the snake to crawl through. You think it was Ali?'

'Nonsense,' said my aunt Hilda who had joined the group just in time to witness the gardener's despatch of the snake. 'You're saying Ali put a cobra in Kit's bed? Sheer nonsense. He's one of the best guides I've ever had. Terribly knowledgeable chap, not to mention trustworthy.'

'Trustworthy!' Ahmed snorted, but I shushed him gently.

'Where is he then?' he went on angrily. 'Where is he, if he is such a fine man?'

The excitement with the snake over, most people had returned to their bedrooms. The hall was empty. Only the boy who slept in the corridor lay curled up on the bare floor. Ahmed strode over to him and questioned him in Arabic. A few minutes later he returned and beckoned us to join him. We climbed a flight of back stairs, not carpeted in red velvet like the front ones, but bare and dingy, and emerged in another corridor. Room number 33. Ahmed tapped on it. There was no answer. He tried the door knob, which opened without resistance.

'See for yourselves!' he said, standing aside. 'My cousin's room.'

A curtain fluttered in the breeze from the wide open window. The bed was dishevelled, blankets and sheets pushed to one side and spilling on to the floor. The basin from the washstand had tipped over, water collected in a puddle under it. Of valises and suitcases, of clothes and personal possessions, there was no sign. Except for one polished leather shoe, which half protruded from the pile of bedclothes. Someone had cleared out in a hurry, judging by the way they had forgotten a fine shoe.

Why had Ali tried to murder me, if indeed he had placed the cobra in my net? He didn't know me, had no grudge against me. If Ali was the culprit he must be working for someone else. Like the Baker Brothers. But why had he disappeared like this? Surely the logical thing was for the villains to have left him here to spy on us. Unless he was scared that Ahmed had unmasked him. My head was full of questions, a cloud of buzzing gnats.

'Now do you believe me?' Ahmed said, staring my aunt fiercely in the face. 'This man Ali, he betrayed my father, his own flesh and blood. He would think nothing of murdering Kit.'

❧ Chapter Twenty-seven ❧

'Zis is ze only life.' Monsieur Champlon smiled back at me on my old donkey, struggling to keep up as his stallion cantered smoothly over the golden sands. 'Ze nomad way, it speaks to ze soul.'

'If you enjoy torturing yourself,' I muttered. How I longed for my own pony, Jesse. Trust my aunt to make sure she and Champlon rode Arab steeds while us 'children' had donkeys. We had been riding through the desert since dawn and were finally approaching Memphis. Dust was irritating my eyes, I was parched and my head was throbbing. The heat was so relentless as we trotted towards our destination, I felt I was being roasted in some celestial furnace.

While my friends and I sweltered and suffered, the Frenchman, Ahmed and my aunt, were taking the pace in their stride. Monsieur Champlon in his pale flowing robes, turban wound magnificently over his head like a large red and yellow pillow, looked as if he had been born to this life.

'You enjoy?' Champlon went on.

'Of course Kit is enjoying it. She's a Salter!' my aunt boomed, turning back on her fine mare. 'Why, this is hardly proper desert at all. Just a little canter through the dunes, if you ask me.'

'I'm having the time of my life,' I said firmly. I did not want to give my aunt any cause for pitying remarks. 'It's magnificent.'

Magnificent our trip had truly been, through the rim of Cairo past the great pyramids of Giza, to which we had given scarcely a glance as we sped by on our mounts. How I wished we could stop. The pyramids. The last one remaining of the seven ancient wonders of the world. The Hanging Gardens of Babylon, the Colossus of Rhodes may have vanished in the sea of time, but the mighty pyramids still remain. What did I feel as I first saw them? Incredible as it might seem, I was a bit disappointed. You see, I had imagined them so many times that when I first glimpsed them it was something of an anti-climax. Almost like paper boxes buried in a child's sandbox.

To tell the truth though, we scarcely got a good impression. Just a snatched glance as we rode past. I'll come back to you, I promised the pyramids. Your mysteries shall not be forever hidden to me.

243

Finally we reached Memphis and again there was the sense of anti-climax.

'*This* is it?' I asked, joining the others in dismounting from my donkey. Champlon offered me a swig of water from his goatskin and I accepted with gratitude. Foolishly I had drunk all my precious liquid.

'The capital city of the ancient world,' Ahmed said, remaining on his donkey.

'But . . .' I began and stopped.

'Time . . .' Ahmed murmured.

He didn't need to complete his sentence: time was the great destroyer. Where once mighty palaces and temples had stood there was now just a few heaps of rubble. Mud, sand, desolation. In fact the only remnant of former glory, a reminder that Pharaohs once ruled Memphis, were two huge statues lying past a clump of palm trees, face down in pools of mud. The once mighty Colossus of Rameses.

'Can we go on now? My family . . .' Ahmed gestured across the sand, to the distance where we could see the peaks of more pyramids. Sakkara, the graveyard of the old kingdom of Memphis. We knew Ahmed's family lived just past it, in a small village.

'Of course,' Isaac said, hurriedly remounting the rather frisky donkey he had been given. Even though we were all weary and needed to stretch our legs, we understood. Finally so close to home, Ahmed must be desperate to see his father.

There were several more miles of hard riding before we neared Sakkara. Our Egyptian friend had sped up his pace as he neared home, ignoring the peak of the Sakkara pyramids, ignoring the urchins who ran after us selling their 'antiques'. They thrust scarabs and other treasures at us, even trying to get in front of our horses, but Ahmed yelled at them and they scattered. This vast graveyard stretched for miles around us. We could see that the earth was littered with shards of ancient pottery, bits of bones and a spongy substance, which according to my aunt was the decayed stumps of mummies.

Sand and ancient flesh were crunching under our horses' feet. We were riding over ancient bones.

Ahmed let out a whoop of joy. Finally he was home: a lush Nile-watered village of mud huts and modest stone dwellings. On the outskirts there rose a handsome house. Shining with fresh whitewash, adorned by curved windows and balconies intricately carved in wood. Its front was sheltered by rows of palms, their long necks swaying gently in the breeze. As we came closer we could see that the windows were shuttered, the whole house wore a forlorn air.

'Something is wrong.' Ahmed halted his horse outside the gate. Suddenly he was ashen-faced.

'You're nervous, that's all.' I tried to soothe him.

'My darling . . . Pepi . . .' Ahmed's voice trailed into a whisper.

'Who is –' I began, thinking perhaps he was mentioning some brother or friend I had not heard of, but he cut me off.

'My best friend. My hunting dog, Pepi. He is an Arabian Saluki. He always comes out barking like a mad thing. Nothing can stop him. He has a sense for my return. Turn back, Kit, I beg you . . . and you, Miss Salter. This is no place for ladies . . . Please.'

'We're not ladies, we're your friends. Whatever happens, Ahmed, we are with you.' I was wasting my breath. Ahmed wasn't listening. He pushed open the gate which was hanging brokenly off the latch. Without a backwards glance, he strode towards the house. I believed, just then, he had forgotten our existence.

'Come on,' I said to the others. Waldo and Isaac followed me along with my aunt, who seemed scarcely bothered, as she trotted behind us.

'A nice 'ouse zis,' Champlon said, pausing by a bush that covered the wall and was absolutely packed with blossoms that looked like wisps of bright pink tissue paper. 'Built of ze t'ick, solid limestone. I stayed in an 'ouse like zis in T'ebes. It vas perfectly cool in ze afternoon.'

'Try and think of other people for once,' I snapped and then I saw something that made me stop in my tracks. Lying half concealed by the flowering bush was an animal. A dog. Blood trickled from the bullet wound in its back to form a puddle under its haunches. Kneeling down, I touched it with the tip of my finger. The dog, a lean hunter, had died recently enough for its fur to be still warm. This must be Pepi, Ahmed's beloved dog.

A presentiment of danger surged through me. Shouting out at the top of my voice I raced to grab my friend and pull him back outside. My fingers closed on air. Ahmed had already pushed open the front door and disappeared inside his home.

❧ Chapter Twenty-eight ❧

Waldo shouldered ahead of me as I tried to follow Ahmed. The door banged behind us, blocking out all but a glimmer of light. We caught up with Ahmed as he entered the living room. It had been ransacked; shards of pottery over the floors, rugs torn to shreds, books turned out of their shelves and scattered. The stuffing of chairs had been ripped out and the wood itself smashed to smithereens. Not a single ornament or piece of furniture had been left unbroken.

A human tornado had blown through here.

Ahmed muttered to himself; he had forgotten us and was speaking in Arabic. He hurried out of the room back into the corridor. As we followed a shot rang out, missing Waldo by a hair's breadth. I dived down and Waldo flattened himself against the wall. Only Ahmed remained where he was, frozen, as if he didn't understand the language of bullets. Another shot rang out. This time it was wildly off target and embedded itself in the ceiling.

'The stairs,' Waldo hissed.

An ebony banister curled up the centre of the house. I could see the gunfire was coming from a shadowy figure on the landing.

'I'll try and crawl over there. See if I can surprise them.' The corridor was so dark I felt sure the gunman was just firing wildly.

'No!' Ahmed said.

'I'm the smallest,' I insisted. 'I'll have the best chance.'

Our friends outside must have had heard the shots. Monsieur Champlon always carried his pistol. As I started to crawl along the floor I was praying he would find a way in, that he would save us.

'I can't let you do this,' Ahmed whispered to me. Then he stepped out from the shadows into the centre of the passage where he was haloed by a faint rim of light. Very slowly he lifted his hands above his head in a gesture of surrender:

'Do not hurt my friends. I am Ahmed El Kassul. Son of Sheikh Mustapha El Kassul. It is me you want.'

Without warning, the pistol clattered down, landing almost in front of my nose. Quick as a flash I reached out, grabbed it and rose up, holding it steady. I swear to you I was ready to fire, but what I saw made no sense to me. An old lady in a black headscarf stood on the landing, tottering against the wall. Her jittery hands had clearly dropped the pistol. As I watched , bewildered, she almost fell down the stairs. Tears were coursing down her cheeks. She collapsed at Ahmed's feet in a crumpled heap.

'My mother,' he explained to us as he bent down and gently scooped her up. His arms closed around her and I saw he was crying as well.

This was a private moment. Waldo and I should not be here. We retreated back into the ransacked room, leaving Ahmed and his mother to their embrace.

'The poor old dame,' Waldo said, looking around for a moment at the scene of devastation. 'She probably thought the villains who did this had come back for more. She must have panicked. She was a menace with that gun.'

'More of a danger to herself than anything. Still, she was very brave.'

Waldo nodded but we were not left long to our reflections because my aunt appeared, Champlon and Isaac in her wake.

'Goodness, they could do with a spot of redecoration!' my aunt said, staring around at the awful mess. She bent down and picked up a broken picture frame, which had contained a piece of Arabic writing.

'I 'eard shooting, is zis not so?' Champlon asked.

I explained about Ahmed's mother. I believed the Velvet Mob must have been here before us. This quietened even my aunt and it was while we were all standing there, feeling subdued and helpless that Ahmed turned up at the door, his eyes red-rimmed from weeping. He came to me and spoke softly in my ear. I nodded and with a quick explanation to the others followed him.

Mustapha El Kassul's bedchamber was on the second floor of the house, a simple, white-washed room cooled by breezes flowing through the arched window. He was lying in a low bed, propped up against the head-board. This room had also been ransacked. Tiny wisps of feathers were everywhere, in clumps on the floor, a few fluttering in the air. The explanation lay by the bed; a heap of shredded pillows.

Looking upon Ahmed's father I felt a thrill of recognition. As if I knew that bony face. Of course he was very like his son, but that wasn't it. I had glimpsed him before, looming out of a puddle of spilt water in the medium's parlour. A fresh bruise ran down one side of the old man's skeletal face. It was livid, beginning to turn purple. Someone had hit him and very hard. Someone who clearly had no respect for old age or the sickness so clear upon his face. It seemed that Mustapha had only woken up from his coma the day before yesterday, about the time we set foot in Egypt and the scarab returned to its native soil. Foolishly I expected Ahmed's father to speak no English, but he was fluent in my language, though with more of a pronounced accent than his son:

'Welcome, Miss Kit, my son has told me how you have helped him.'

'Thank you.'

'You have been a good and true friend to him at a time when he needed this support, more than anything else. For that I am truly grateful. My friend . . .' Mustapha fell silent, struggling to sit up. His son took his elbow and gently helped him up.

'We have always been fortunate in our son. Even when he has been reckless I know that he will never do what is wrong . . . when I depart Ahmed will be the head of the family.'

'No.' Ahmed burst out angrily. 'Now you are well again I will not hear this talk.'

'It is not talk my boy, it is a fact. I have only been granted a short visit in this life. I know this for sure and you will have to face it. Very soon, maybe only days, I will be gone. I am not going to tell you that I have no fear of this . . .' he paused a moment, and that moment was only for his son. 'I have had a long life . . . a good one.'

Ahmed bent his head.

'A heavy burden. I know you Ahmed, you will bear it well. Now, my boy, I want to talk of something else: Ptah Hotep.'

'His scarab,' I burst out, though it would have been more polite to hold my tongue. 'We know it is the clue to treasure.'

'Of sorts.'

'Gold?'

'Something far more valuable.'

'Diamonds?'

'Words.'

'Words? But words aren't treasure!'

'Wisdom is a treasure, Miss Kit. The words Ptah Hotep had inscribed all those millennia ago are more precious than diamonds to those who value wisdom. How do you feel after words of anger are uttered? Does not the very air around you change? Does not the heart sink? As words of evil spread misery, words of wisdom bring enchantment to our lives.

'As my son may have told you, Ptah Hotep was not just a vizier to the Pharaoh. More importantly he was a great sage, one whose wisdom has lived on in Egypt, handed down over the ages from father to son. His flame has burnt for many, many centuries keeping all of us warm. For countless generations our family have faithfully carried out a sacred task to preserve Ptah Hotep's soul according to the traditions of the ancients.'

'But the scarab . . . the mummy . . . it is all gone,' Ahmed whispered.

'Yes, the mummy is gone and so is the scarab but not all is lost. Centuries ago my ancestors moved the book – the magical book – in which Ptah Hotep set down his thoughts.'

The old man in the midst of the wreckage of his room should have been a pitiful sight. Our talk, however, had re-kindled the blaze inside him and his eyes were bright. Hard to believe this was the same, dying man I had seen huddled in his bed a few minutes ago.

'I am telling you of the *oldest book in the world!*

'Just imagine. Thousand of years before the birth of Jesus. Before Mohammed, before Buddha, before all the sages who men around the world revere. This, my son, is our link with the very dawn of man's time on earth. This is what those villains want. The secret hiding place of the *World's Oldest Book.*

In a flash it all made sense to me. That was why the Baker Brothers were studying my father's scholarly work. The ancient manuscript Papa had mentioned, the Papyrus Prisse, was a mere copy of the world's oldest book. It was inscribed thousands of years after Ptah Hotep's death and was only a pale reflection of the genuine article. We knew nothing of the contents of the real papyrus, but the legend surrounding it spoke of wonders beyond compare. What would really drive men like the Bakers, who had all the gold and diamonds they could ever want? What did they yearn to possess?

'They did not care who they destroyed to seek this Book of Wonder and Wisdom, this book that can confer blessings and curses,' the old man's croaking voice continued. 'Why such people seek to possess this book I do not know. They will never truly understand it with such greed in their hearts.'

'They will rot for ever,' Ahmed's mother burst out. 'The mummy's curse is upon them.'

'The mummy's curse?' I echoed, remembering how Ahmed had said the loss of the scarab had cursed his village.

'Superstition,' his father said.

'Stop!' Ahmed's mother burst out. Her headscarf had fallen away revealing wild white hair. 'Curse is TRUE!'

Mustapha turned to his wife and spoke to her in Arabic. She nodded her head, somewhat sullenly, and fell silent.

'Who were the people who did this to you?' I ventured nervously.

The old man shrugged, indifferently. 'Lost souls.'

'Fat woman her skin like sour cream,' Ahmed's mother

burst out, unstoppable. 'She order everyone and they beat Ahmed's father. And there is two white ghost men who do nothing, they just look. The fat one she is evil I can see it. She will destroy anything. They are going to kill Ahmed's father so I agree. They show me scarab and I talk. I read the clues on scarab. I tell where book is buried.'

'Where?' I asked.

'Siwa. I say nothing else because I cannot tell anything else. They satisfied, they go.'

'It is an oasis in the wilderness of the Western desert,' Ahmed muttered. 'It will take them weeks to trek there, if they are able to make it. I do not believe any Englishman has ever travelled there.'

'Will they be able to find the book's hiding place?' I asked Ahmed's father anxiously. 'Is it possible, if all they know is Siwa?'

There was no answer. Ahmed's father had sunk back on his bed, where he lay gazing vacantly at the ceiling. His flame had dimmed, he looked what he was: an old man very close to death. 'Who knows?' he murmured. 'When they moved the book my ancestors engraved a clue in the scarab. If they can read this, who knows?'

It was time to go. I could see my departure in Ahmed's sad face. At the door I turned back and took one more look at Sheikh Mustapha El Kassul, knowing in my very bones that it would be the last time I saw him.

✏ Chapter Twenty-nine ✏

We left the village before the muezzin's call to prayers, well before first light. Ahmed and a young Berber man, who was said to be the best tracker in the tribe, went first. Waldo, Isaac, Champlon, my aunt and I followed in a straggling line, bumping up and down on our own camels. Bringing up the rear were five tribesmen, accompanied by ten camels weighed down with water-skins and food. All of the men were prepared to fight for us, Ahmed had assured us. As we set off for the fabled oasis in the desert I reflected that we were now a true caravanserai – following in the footsteps of the merchant parties who had journeyed through these trackless wastes for centuries.

My aunt trotted beside me as the sun rose, dusting the sand dunes with a pink blush. As you can imagine, she was in her element. She had chosen to dress as a desert Arab, a flowing white robe, a scarf tied around her head, simple sandals. I had been happy to follow her lead for the male robes looked loose and comfortable.

'Good to finally get some decent exploring in,' Aunt Hilda grunted.

'Has anyone, any English explorer I mean, ever been to Siwa?' I asked.

'I think the world's first true account of Siwa will be from Hilda Salter.'

'And Gaston Champlon,' the Frenchman put in.

'Of course, monsieur,' my aunt said, with a twinkle. 'I wasn't thinking of the French. I meant the English-Speaking World!'

What can I tell you of our desert ride? Imagine a huge space, bigger than your home town, bigger than England herself. Imagine this space is built purely of sand, a vast ocean of the stuff. Dunes rise and fall but all is bare and there is scarcely a bit of a tree, bush or living thing to be seen. I was told that our guides could tell one dune from another. I sincerely hoped so, for to me one heap of sand looked much like another and there is no road through the desert. My description might sound very grim but that is not the whole picture. I swear to you there is beauty here: the golden sands; the fantastic shapes whipped up by the wind; the stunning ridges of salt – but my gosh it is a very bleak sort of beauty.

By the end of the first day's hard riding my eyes were again red from the fine stream of sand that irritated them, despite my headscarf. Breathing was a trial because the hot air dried out the membranes of my nose and made every breath a fiery torture. My throat ached with longing for a drink but Ahmed had warned us we had to ration our water most carefully. The way through the desert was perilous. If we did not conserve our food and water and even more crucially find some pasture for our camels to feed, we could easily die here under the merciless sun. Egyptians believe that in the desert a camel's welfare is more important than its owner's. Camels can survive at the very most for two weeks without food, living off the fat stores in their humps, but if they sicken and die then their masters are truly done for!

Even Champlon and my aunt were tiring as the days wore on. Only Ahmed and his men seemed to be thriving. In his desert costume: turban, striped gown, coloured scarves wound round his waists jangling with pistols and knives, Ahmed looked like a bandit prince. Even though at thirteen years old he was the youngest of them, the men of his Berber tribe respected his authority. I gathered that his father Sheikh El Kassul commanded respect from all these men and I was glad of it, because we were truly in the wilds journeying where few westerners had ever set foot. Our lives depended on Ahmed's men and they in turn on their camels.

At times, I confess, my heart sank and my spirits were

weak. Waldo I knew was going through the same thing. As for Isaac, he had bottled it all up again and it was hard to know what he was thinking. Why had we ever volunteered for this hardship? And then I thought of Rachel, travelling through the desert with another caravan and my heart was stronger. If not for the Book and the scarab – love for my friend would give me the strength to endure this journey.

By the end of the tenth day all of us had toughened up a little. I had learned to wind my scarf low over my eyebrows so as to keep out the sand and grit. I had learned to breathe evenly, despite the pain in my nostrils. I was even starting to enjoy the camel riding having learnt not to sit astride the beast, which makes your thighs ache, but perch with my legs wrapped around the front hump. Maybe I was becoming more of a desert explorer because I was even starting to be able to tell the difference between various types of dunes and to spot where a water-course might lie. We spotted gazelles, desert rats and hares. My favourite part of each day, however, was the evening when we unsaddled, set up our simple cloth tents and cooked a frugal meal over a camp fire.

Tonight, after existing for too many days on bread smeared with a little butter, we were going to feast. Clever Ahmed had pulled a hare out of a bush. One of the men roasted it whole over the fire to preserve the precious juices and we ate it ravenously, soaking up the sauce with bread. I lay down after our feast, looking at the orb of the moon, hanging lower and closer than ever at home. I felt I could reach out my hand and pluck it, like a silver apple. The men were singing some wailing desert song round the camp fire. It was wild and eerie but not unpleasant.

I felt strangely at peace.

'Ghazou! Ghazou!' harsh cries broke into my reverie.

One man jumped up and stamped on the fire, scattering burning embers in a wide arc. Others leapt up drawing swords and pistol. 'A raid,' Ahmed hissed. 'Quick back to the camels.'

'Who are they?'

'Enemies! Quick, with me.'

Shots rang out in the still desert air and I heard the racing of hooves. Before we could retreat the raiders were upon us, racing through our camp in a storm of sand and gunfire. Dark shrouded figures, on fast camels, their faces covered by scarves. As they rode some of them scythed the air with glittering swords. They were after our camels but they were not to have it all their own way. Our men, who a moment before had been singing before the campfire replete with food, had drawn their weapons. All around me was the clashing of swords and the sting of gunfire. I found myself in the middle of a pitched battle.

'Behind me,' hissed Waldo. 'Keep down.' A firearm glittered in his hand. A tall man in a scarlet cloak was heading our way. Waldo fired – but the bullet went wide. The man leant down and slashed at Waldo, expertly sending the gun spinning away into the desert. Blood dripped down Waldo's hand. The raider laughed, showing teeth that gleamed white in the darkness; he kicked out viciously; the blow hit Waldo hard in the chest and sent him toppling into the sand.

It was Ali, Ahmed's treacherous cousin.

'No!' I yelled, diving down. I had some idea I could upset the rider by attacking his steed; instead I fell perilously close to the camel's legs. The next few seconds were a blur, something walloped me hard in the head making my world go dizzy, then I felt strong hands pulling me back. It was Waldo. Or was it Champlon? Hard to tell in the melee of bodies and swords.

'Thanks,' I gasped scrambling out of the camel's way.

Champlon was smiling. Calmly he raised his gun, levelled his sights, took aim and fired. The bullet grazed the raider's arm, just as it was upstretched to catch Waldo another blow. Stunned, Ali howled in pain and dropped his sword, which fell in the sand. I dived to catch it, getting there just a second before Waldo.

I grabbed it and was about to stab the traitor – but he was gone; racing out of our camp on his camel, as fast as his whip could spur the beast.

All around us raiders were charging, but Champlon was a marvel. The calm eye of the storm, he stood straight and still, sending shot after shot straight to its targets. A bullet hit a raider's sword, causing it to fly out of his hands. Another smacked into a the shoulder of a man with a sweeping moustache; his yowl rose above the noise of the attack like a jackal's wail.

The raiders hadn't expected Champlon; a human hailstorm of bullets. We were armed, more aggressive in our own defence than might have been expected. Through the sand, we saw the raiders in retreat. Not before they had gained some precious plunder. One had got away with a saddlebag full of food, another with a tent, a third swiped a camel and was racing away, goading the reluctant beast with sticks and prods.

'Leave them!' Ahmed ordered his men, who were about to jump on their own camels and pursue the raiders.

'Piffle. I will see to them myself.' My reckless aunt jumped on her camel and rode off after the raiders.

'Champlon will never desert you!' The Frenchman followed closely. Before Ahmed could order them to their senses, the two adults had disappeared over a sand dune, chasing the raiders in the star-spangled darkness. They would surely get lost. One sand dune is much like another to my aunt, however much familiarity with the desert she claims.

'We must bring them back!' I cried, rushing to my camel. 'This is madness!'

'Stay!' Ahmed said. 'We will track them tomorrow at first light. It will be impossible tonight.' I could see his point for they had already been swallowed up by the night. The raiders were gone and sudden silence descended on the camp; eerie after the panic of the raid. Then from the remains of the campfire we heard a loud shout in Arabic, followed by a clamour of voices.

'What is it?' I asked, fearful of more raiders.

'They have caught a hostage!' Ahmed explained.

We hurried to the spot where a small, slight Arab was struggling in the clutches of two of our strongest men. He was dressed in shabby robes, had a dark villainous face and was yelling loudly as we approached. English words were mixed in with his moans! There was something familiar about the man, though for a moment I couldn't place what it was. Then I leant forward and wiped at his face with a finger I had moistened with spit. The grit and dirt peeled off, revealing pale, reddish skin.

❧ Chapter Thirty ❧

'Jabber!' I exclaimed.

'Pleased to meet yer again, Kit.'

'Is it really you?' I asked, staring at his dirty, tanned face, topped by that mop of carroty hair.

'Course it's me. Who do yer think it is? Me Arab double? I'm too gorgeous for that, I am. They don't build men like Jabber Jukes out 'ere in these hot countries.'

'What are you doing here?' I ignored this typical piece of arrogance.

'I'm on 'oliday.'

'Be serious, Jabber.'

'Wot do yer think? I'm wiv the Velvet Mob.'

'And we captured you . . .'

'Not likely.'

'What do you mean?'

'Let's just say I decided to stay behind and have a little rest when the Velvets scarpered.'

Egyptian life had treated Jabber well. He was wearing smart robes, a headscarf and around his waist a bandolier of bullets. He positively jangled with weapons. How smoothly my East End friend had transformed from a whippersnapper of an English thug to an Oriental one. Then it occurred to me:

'Rachel?'

He nodded, sagely: 'I done all I could for her.'

'How is she? How are they treating her?'

Waldo, holding his bloody hand in the crook of his arm, and Isaac had come close, attracted by the din. They watched in amazement as our old friend was revealed. Jabber was completely surrounded by the hostile crowd, his grubby face faintly lit by the glow of scattered embers. He should have been fearful, but being Jabber he was cocky instead.

'Jabber! I asked you about Rachel!'

'She's all right.'

'It must be terrible for poor Rachel. Surrounded by enemies. Not knowing if help is going to come. Oh my poor friend.'

'I'll kill 'em. When I find those thugs I'll kill them.' Isaac burst out and Waldo put a comforting arm around his shoulder, even though he was wincing with pain.

'Do they drug her, Jabber?' I asked. 'We heard that at Shepheard's Hotel she was drugged?'

'I 'ad to give her sumfink to make her sleep. You got a lot to be grateful to Uncle Jabber for. It was me wot looked after the little lady, I –' He broke off stunned, his hand rising to protect his face where Ahmed had just walloped him.

'Wotcha do that for?'

Ahmed let loose again, giving Jabber another resounding slap. 'You do not drug a lady!' he shouted, his face purple with rage.

The men took this as an invitation to pile in – and in a flash Jabber was attacked from all sides. They were going to make mincemeat out of him.

'STOP!' I roared. 'This boy can help us. He can tell us about Rachel and help us to find her.'

'Yeah, Kit's right,' Jabber whined. 'I tell yer I 'elped Rachel. I'll 'elp yer find 'er. What do you think I'm 'ere for?'

'He's not to be trusted,' Ahmed hissed. 'He may be a spy. Let me beat the truth out of him.'

'No! Jabber is my *friend*. He will help us, Ahmed. You have my word on it.'

My word alone had to satisfy them. Grumbling, the men returned to try and catch a little sleep before dawn. Ahmed took Waldo away to treat the slash on the top of his hand, Isaac trudging away with them. Not before Ahmed had given me a very dirty look and Isaac had informed me it was on my head; if Jabber betrayed us it would be my fault.

'You heard what Isaac said,' I said to Jabber, squatting by the cinders of wood for their remnants of warmth, because early dawn can be bitterly cold in the desert. He had the grace to look ashamed. We had a long chat then, and what he told me about Rachel went some way to reassure me. It sounded like Jabber had been a friend to her, trying to make sure the mob treated her decently, even promising that he would help her escape if the chance came. Not that it ever had, because Rachel was always well guarded. I had a hunch his information would prove vital and I was grateful for it.

It was hard next morning to saddle up the camels and be on our way; not knowing where Champlon and my aunt had taken it upon themselves to go, not knowing of Rachel's fate. Our tracker guide soon picked up Champlon's and Aunt Hilda's tracks. We followed the two of them for several hours, only to discover they themselves were following the raiders. According to our guide, the raiders had been a party of seven men, including three Westerners, one of them a lady. Later tracks and camel droppings showed they met up with another party, a well-stocked one with thirty baggage camels and another ten men, two of them foreigners. How he could tell that by marks in the sand don't ask me. Apparently

Englishmen sit differently on their camels! It looked like the Baker Brothers and Velvet Nell were travelling through this harsh desert in the style of emperors.

We didn't stop for lunch, just moistened our parched throats with a little brackish liquid which we had found in the last watering hole. It was one of our usual days in the desert, sand, sand and more sand. Then suddenly a joyful cry went up from the men. We were in sight of Siwa!

'Where?' I asked.

In front of us stretched a large salt ridge, nothing more. More sand dunes on all sides. I expected some sort of mirage, at the very least. A few days ago I had seen a lake – wonderfully, liquidly blue. In my excitement I'd galloped towards it, hollering with glee, which made the men rock with laughter. What a foolish foreigner I was! Those deliciously cool waters turned out to be nothing but an illusion!

'Where's Siwa?' chimed in Waldo and Ahmed.

The men chattered in Arabic and Ahmed listened. Then he turned to us with a smile. 'Your aunt and Champlon, they are following the Velvet Mob. But my tracker, he knows a secret way. We will beat those villains to our oasis!'

Instead of labouring over those salt ridges till our camels' feet were sore and we were dripping with sweat, we took a very clever route. Behind a large rock was a tunnel hollowed out of salt. We had to dismount from our camels, because the roof was so low, but it was beautifully cool inside. We moved at a steady pace, careful not to knock our heads on the stalactites which dripped down from the roof of the tunnel. Our camels didn't like it, we had to prod them to persuade them onwards, but for us it was a refreshing change from the glare of sand and sun and the relentless heat. When we had emerged from the tunnel, the sun seemed hotter than ever. For the first time on our journey I felt I simply couldn't bear it any longer. So it was lucky that soon after we arrived at the most splendid sight in the world! There is nothing – nothing – to compare with the vision of an oasis after weeks in the desert.

Under a gleaming hilltop citadel, hewn out of white salt rock, nestled the most adorable little town. Chalky houses. Trees of apricot, palm and olive. Bubbling springs. A cool blue lake, which I longed to swim in. Never, ever had I seen a more beautiful sight. Why, the pyramids were nothing compared to this. It was positively brimming with life. So must the Garden of Eden have looked to Adam and Eve!

'The Book is hidden here,' I said to Ahmed, as we sat on our camels looking at this vision.

'Yes.' He nodded. 'Siwa has always been a special

place to my Berber people. Here we were safe and free when the Arabs invaded Egypt all those centuries ago.'

'Your father thought the Mob may have learnt the secret hiding place. How are we going to stop the Baker Brothers finding the treasure?' I asked.

Ahmed didn't seem to be listening to me. He patted his camel's satiny flank, causing the beast to swivel its head so it was looking out over Siwa. Then, as if it sensed water and life, the camel broke into a trot. As we glided over the sands towards our desert oasis, Ahmed grinned at me:

'The cactus blooms in the desert.'

'What *are* you talking about?'

'We are Berbers, the desert is in our blood and bones. We are not scared of her, she is our friend.'

'So?'

'Don't worry. I have a plan!'

❧ Chapter Thirty-one ❧

'If you would be so kind, Mr Baker,' I said.

I moved closer to the man, feeling as if I was stepping up to a statue made of ice. He was dressed in a flawless white linen suit, his face hiding in the shadow of his palm-leaf hat. His skin was papery, his eyes flat – they could have been bits of glass in the face of a Punch and Judy puppet. I didn't know which brother he was, but at that moment I didn't care. I grabbed the front of his jacket. There it was, something heavy sewn into the silk lining. Something that made the jacket hang wrong. So I must have picked the right Baker! A quick slash with my knife and the thing tumbled into my hand.

A smooth shining black beetle, its body carved with ancient symbols. The cause of all our trouble. The scarab.

'Thank you,' I murmured.

Mr Baker looked at me expressionlessly. His brother, in identical linen suit, equally blank by his side. They may have appeared a couple of puppets but I knew they were furious. I felt the chill coming off them and for a second I feared for Ahmed, who had a gun to the other brother's neck.

Ahmed's men had executed the ambush with the skill of trained desert soldiers. We had waited for the Velvet Mob, camouflaged behind rocks at the bend of the path to Siwa. They came, noisy and chatting, excited to be at the oasis at last. They had no reason to be fearful, no reason to think we had set them a trap. They walked blindly into the fine silken nets we had spread over the road. Camels reared, men tumbled. Chaos and panic on all sides. Before our enemies had a chance to react we were in amongst them, our weapons at the ready. The Velvet Mob were bigger and better armed than us, but we had the advantage of surprise and organisation. I admit I did have a moment's doubt about Jabber, but he fought bravely, catching Bender Barney a blow that sent him flying against the rocks. Jabber's information had been vital in securing the scarab – and his knowledge of the Velvet's set-up enabled us to fight this battle, swift and sure. Now the rats were well and truly in our trap.

Only one riddle remained: where was Rachel?

'Rachel!' I called, adding my voice to Isaac and

Ahmed's. We searched in vain among the villains and their hired Arab guards. Hopeless. There was no sign of her.

'If you've hurt her,' Isaac blurted out, losing control.

There was a rustling within the Velvet ranks. With a swoosh of her finery, Velvet Nell emerged from behind a camel and stood before us, magnificent in a satin cloak of the deepest scarlet. Her lips matched the colour of her cloak, a cruel red slash in her creamy skin.

'You want your little friend?' she purred.

'What have you done with her?' I replied, struggling to control my temper.

'You *really* want her back?'

'You witch!'

'She's far more trouble than she's worth. I've never met such a milksop. Well, there's no accounting for taste, I suppose. Here you are.'

Velvet Nell, moved slightly to the side. I saw that she was holding an Arab girl dressed from head to toe in black, eyes veiled. Below the veil I could see a gag, bound tight about her mouth. The girl squirmed in Nell's grip. It was Rachel looking out from behind that veil.

'If you want her, you'll have to give me something in return,' Nell said.

Nell had a pistol to Rachel's head. Isaac screamed and

jostled Ahmed, whose hand trembled. The hand holding the gun which had a Baker Brother hostage. They may have looked like wrung-out dishcloths but it seemed the Brothers could be fighters. This brother jumped, flicking the gun down into the sand. In the blink of an eye we had lost our advantage.

'No!' I shouted.

'I'm afraid so, me dear.'

Nell stuck out a fleshy hand, its fingers dripping blood-coloured talons. 'I'll take the scarab, if you please.'

I closed my hands over the scarab, my mind racing to think how I could save it – and Rachel. If I could somehow distract Nell, throw the scarab into the sand . . . but I had no time, for a furious bundle closed in on me. Shrieking in fury it took the scarab from my clutches and threw it at Nell.

'Take the bloomin' thing!' Isaac shouted. 'Just give me my sister back.'

Nell caught the scarab mid-air and her hand curled round it lovingly. Then with a rough shove she pushed Rachel forward, into Isaac's arms.

'You got the worst of the bargain,' Velvet Nell said.

Meanwhile Ahmed had kept his head in the confusion, diving down and retrieving his gun. Now pointed it at a Baker Brother, but another Brother held a gun to him. I looked around in confusion. Both sides were armed to the teeth, weapons sprouting everywhere I looked.

'It seems we could take you all.' Nell smiled.

'Or we could take you!' Ahmed snapped.

A stalemate. Or a bloody massacre. One of the Baker Brothers motioned Velvet Nell to come to him. She listened to his instructions, then spoke to us:

'My employer, he doesn't want mess and questions. So he says, let's call it quits.'

'Fine!' Ahmed replied, keeping firm hold of his gun.

'Mr Baker says, don't bother to follow us. It's against his principles to fight children – but you are making yourselves an awful nuisance and he is sorely tempted to give you all a good hiding. Now you sit tight here while we leave. All right? Just to make sure you keep your word like good little children, we'll leave Bender and Ali here to cover you.'

Bender and Ali stayed behind on their camels as our enemies remounted their steeds. Ahmed had seen Ali too and glowered at the man who had betrayed his family. There was one bright spot, though. Bender had acquired a black eye in the fight! It was all we could do to stay our men's hands as their caravanserai moved off in a flurry of trotting legs and waving guns. We watched them go, round the bend into the town of Siwa. Finally

Bender and Ali followed, not before the latter had given his cousin a particularly unpleasant smirk. The villains were gone – for the time being at least.

Rachel unpeeled herself from Isaac and was mumbling something. Her dark eyes flashed above her gag as she writhed.

'Pardon?' Isaac said, looking at his sister in confusion.

'She can't talk, idiot,' I said. I bounded towards Rachel and peeled off her gag.

Words tumbled out as soon as the material was removed. Angry, bitter words. This was a new Rachel:

'Don't follow them,' she spat. 'Let the rats go.'

Ahmed came up to her and gently took her hand in his. As he did I saw a trace of the old softness return to Rachel's eyes. I wondered about her ordeal and hoped that it had not damaged her kind spirit.

'Don't worry,' he murmured. 'We won't follow them.'

'Then where?' Rachel's hand trembled in his.

'Our hope, our only hope now, is to get to the Book before them.'

❧ Chapter Thirty-two ❧

'You're sure your ancestors hid the Book here?' I asked, hugging myself for comfort. I was unable to get rid of the strong feeling that I wanted to be somewhere, anywhere, else.

'Quiet,' Ahmed murmured. 'It does not do to speak of such things.'

Ancient stone walls surrounded us, cracked and crumbling. Strange hieroglyphics adorned the walls and even odder drawings: a crown, a floating limb, vases of wine, the profile of a god. The sun blazed out of a blue sky on the gaping roof of the temple, but the place was strangely gloomy. Waldo shuffled by my side, his unease infecting me.

'Do you know what an Oracle is?' Ahmed asked.

'She was a priestess in the ancient world, usually a young woman of noble birth,' I answered. 'The ancients believed she was the mouthpiece of the gods. They believed she could foretell the future.'

'One of the mightiest Oracles in the world dwelt here . . .'

We looked around us, the desolation of glory, the odd heathen animals and gods on the ruined walls. It was easy to believe that wonder beyond imagining had dwelt here.

'Alexander the Great, the mighty Greek warrior, came here many centuries ago,' Ahmed was whispering, as if fearful of being overheard. 'He begged the Oracle's favour. She told him he was the rightful Pharaoh and he went on to become King of Egypt. The Oracle did not bless others. Over two thousand years ago, Cambyses the Persian invader threatened to destroy the Oracle because she would not tell him he was the true ruler of Egypt. He sent six thousand soldiers to ransack this place but they all vanished in a sandstorm. Were they buried alive in the desert? Did they flee from some supernatural terror? No one knows because centuries later, to this day, not a single trace of them has been found.'

'An oracle couldn't make a whole army disappear,' Isaac said. 'I mean, this place is strange, but oracles and all, it's hardly science, is it?'

'The power of the Oracle is so great that only a fool would ignore it,' Ahmed replied.

It was just the five of us: Rachel, Ahmed, Isaac,

Waldo and I. Ahmed had not wanted to let anyone else into this sacred place, certainly not Jabber. We had left our guides and camels resting. Making absolutely sure we weren't followed, we trekked up to this temple, built on a jutting strip of rock. It was a bleak place. Ahmed told us there were two other temples devoted to the same oracle – but only a very few scholars knew of this place, a ruin on the outskirts of the village, where the Oracle had truly lived. Ordinary people avoided it, because its legend was so forbidding. No Siwan would tell an outsider of its existence on account of the curse.

'No one else must ever see this. No one else must ever know about this,' Ahmed said. He was kneeling down in the corner of the room and now we saw something truly extraordinary. He had pressed some secret lever or chanted some secret code; we did not know what. A section of ground moved away, revealing a series of steps hewn into the rock. It was very dark and impossible to tell how far the steps went.

'We're not going down there?' I asked, my voice unusually squeaky. Despite myself I had visions of being trapped in some underground chamber.

'You can wait up here, all of you, if you please,' Ahmed answered. He took out a stick wrapped in cloth and a packet of matches. Calmly, he lit the brand, which gave off a wavering light.

'No. No. I'm coming with you.'

Rachel, who normally would have been urging caution, had set off down the steps without hesitation. Waldo followed her, then Isaac, while I followed behind, my heart in my mouth. Ahmed's brand gave out just a faint light so we made our way by feeling with our hands and feet. The walls were cold and moist. Down, down we went till we must have descended into the very heart of the mountain. At the bottom of the shaft a tunnel turned to the left, Ahmed went first and then the others. We had to crawl on our hands and knees and there was so little air in here that every inch was painful. Something crunched under my feet, something glowing white.

I screamed and ahead of me Rachel turned.

'What is it, Kit?' she hissed.

'Nothing,' I replied. But I was lying. I knew what I had stepped on. A fragment of old skull, bleached white. So brittle even my light sandals could crush it. Who did they belong to, these ancient bones? A priest? A thief? I had no time for speculation for we had emerged into a soaring cavern, its walls and roof dripping with contortions of rock and salt. Miracle of miracles, the whole chamber was glowing yellow, as if lit by some unearthly glow.

'How?' I asked, looking around in delight.

'The ancients believed it was one of the Oracle's wonders,' Ahmed answered. 'I suppose you, Isaac, would have another explanation?'

'There must be a way sunlight is refracting off a naturally reflective surface,' Isaac mused. 'I wonder where the source of illumination is?'

I looked around at the glowing cavern, here and there the walls flickered bronze, gold, a hint of scarlet. I imagined I was an ancient Egyptian, living near the dawn of man's history. Here I might dream that I had discovered the source of the earth's fire. Here was something to light one's soul.

'I don't always want to believe in science,' I said to Isaac. 'I know this sounds stupid, but sometimes I prefer wonder.'

'There is no greater wonder than science. I mean science might even one day make it possible to build a time machine to take us back to the age of the Pharaohs.'

'That's never going to happen.'

Isaac turned away. Ahmed, taking no notice of us, was looking for the Book. It was nowhere to be seen. No large chest, to protect the World's Oldest Book from damp and dust. No marker stone to indicate where such treasure was buried. Then, at the same time, we *all* saw it. Sitting on a natural ledge, just a little above our heads, something wrapped in a dust-coloured cloth. Something that had blended with the very colour of the desert rocks. Ahmed stretched, his hand extended to take the object . . .

'STOP,' a voice rang out.

We had company. Crawling out of the tunnel, emerging into the cave's amber glow, they came. Velvet Nell, Bender Barney, Ali and finally like two ghosts, the Baker Brothers. They all carried guns in their hands, which they pointed at us.

'You cannot bring guns here,' Ahmed said, his voice trembling with anger. 'This is a sacred place.' To his cousin Ali, he added. 'You of all people should know this.'

'Too much superstition,' Ali leered. 'That was always your father's problem. Now I see you have the family disease.'

'We got the guns, my dear, we make the rules,' Nell snapped.

'Shall I tie 'em up?' Bender Barney asked, clearly itching to get his hands on us.

'Pat 'em down, Bender and Ali,' Nell replied. 'Make sure they ain't armed.' Her beautiful mouth was open in a scarlet smile, showing every one of her pearly teeth. She was radiant, enjoying every minute of this. 'I don't mind admitting I wanted to off the lot of yer, but my employers, they're wise birds. They said leave 'em be.

They'll take us to the Book. They'll lead us right to the treasure if we play 'em right.'

'You are fools,' Ahmed said, then flinched as Ali who was searching him, gave him a casual blow. 'You had the secret if you decoded the scarab.'

'Oi, watch yer mouf!' Bender growled.

'We could have done it,' Ali said. 'I puzzled out the hieroglyphics myself but I wasn't certain. Besides, as I said to Mr Baker, why exert ourselves? Why get into a sweat working out where the Book is hidden when we've got you idiots to sweat for us?'

'ENOUGH TALK!' one of the Baker Brothers had spoken. At least, his mouth moved and words emerged into the cave.

'Take it. We want you to take the *Book*,' the other Brother said to Velvet Nell.

Nell hesitated and Ahmed let out a wail.

'Take it, Nell,' the Brother insisted. 'Take the Book and we will be gone.'

'She mustn't touch it,' Ahmed said. 'She is a non-believer.'

Nell looked at him for a split second. A small nerve was twitching above the curve of her lip, but otherwise her face was beautiful and bland as a marble bust. Then she moved over to the ledge where the Book dwelt. We watched, powerless, as she stood before it, her hand rising. For me, at that moment, it was as if Isaac's imaginary time machine had cast a spell over us all. Every moment was a frozen hour as Velvet Nell rose on her tiptoes and put out her shapely arm to take the Book. She had it. The precious thing lay in her hands, she was unpeeling mouldering layers of cloth, shaking them impatiently to the ground. They fell, disregarded, till the manuscript was revealed.

Jewel-bright hieroglyphics, more precious than diamonds, glowing on ancient papyrus. The wisdom of the dawn – the magic of awakening thought. An age when man was closer to the great natural truths – to the language of bird and beast. Here it was, before us.

'See, nothing but a bit of harmless old paper,' Nell said with a grin.

'Drop it,' Ahmed urged. 'Do not let the Book destroy you.'

'I'm a modern missus,' Nell replied. 'Don't believe in curses and all that old nonsense. Why I –'

Abruptly Nell stopped, panic on her face. Rachel clutched my arm. There was a whistling noise all around us and in the upper reaches of the vast cavern a swirl of sand.

'Khamsin,' Ahmed whispered to us.

I stared at him.

'A sirocco. Desert sandstorm. Cover your mouth and

nose with your scarf else you will choke.'

He showed Rachel how to adjust her scarf while I tried my best to wrap my own around my head. I had heard of the deadly siroccos; blinding men and beasts with knives of sand. The wind could reach fifty miles an hour and build towering castles of sand which hung in the air. It could lash your skin raw. The Bakers, Ali and Bender Barney were moving towards the stairs, unaware. I made to follow them but Ahmed pulled me back.

'We could be buried alive,' I hissed. The cave was thick with golden grains, whipping and careening around us, making it hard to see more than a few feet in any direction.

'Look,' he said, pointing, and everyone turned to look at Nell.

Her body was writhing but her feet, as if glued to the earth, didn't move. She opened her scarlet lips and spat something out. There was a trickle of sand among the spittle. We watched torn between bewilderment and horror. She spat again, more sand. How? Had she been swallowing it? She was vomiting up a stream of the stuff. As we watched, uncomprehending, the sirocco still swirling around us, more and more sand was disgorged from her lips. Was Nell the origin of it all? She choked, her voice desert-dry, struggling to utter a word.

'Help me!' she cried. At least I think that was what she was saying but it was impossible to tell with the sand throttling her words. The grip that held her feet frozen seemed to relax, for now Velvet Nell sank down to the ground, her arms swinging this way and that. She was the flailing centre of a Biblical storm. Sand eddied around her, settling in flurries and mounds. Sand buried her up to her waist. Obsessively her left hand clutched the Book, held just above the rising sea of sand.

'She has insulted the spirits!' Ahmed cried. 'She is a cursed thing.'

To the side, Ali urgently whispered something to one of the Bakers. The Brother moved back from the tunnel and walked up to Ahmed, one hand shielding his eyes from the penetrating sand, the other pointing his gun at our friend.

'Forget her,' The Brother ordered. '*You* get the Book.'

'No. We've got to save the woman. The sand is going to crush her –'

The Brother clicked the safety catch off the pistol and held it to Ahmed's throat: 'Now,' he hissed.

Ahmed obeyed. He was surrounded by sinuous sand snakes that obscured him from my eyes. As for Nell, she had almost vanished. One bare arm poked out from a hill of sand, fingers curled in a death grip around the Book. Rachel ran towards Ahmed, trying to pull him back but he moved like a sleepwalker. I could scarcely see, the sand was in my eyes, stinging my bare arms, cutting my legs so I wanted to scream out.

Ahmed reached out and took the Book from Nell but her lifeless hand gripped it more tightly. He wrenched it away, prising her fingers off it one by one, till her hand flopped and the Book came loose. Gently Ahmed took the papyrus. I had expected Ahmed to be struck, as Nell had, to be suspended in a pillar of sand.

Nothing happened. He was free and now we were all running to the tunnel, stumbling into each other in our haste. Ahmed went first, Ali, the Baker Brothers and Bender Barney bringing up the rear, their guns prodding our backs. We crawled through the tunnel and then up the steps lining the rock shaft, tumbling into the temple upstairs where – another miracle – the sand had gone. The air was clear and fresh. Sunlight blazed through the ruined roof – apart from the gentlest of breezes all was still. Hard to believe that down below a devilry of sand had claimed the life of Velvet Nell.

The Baker Brothers emerged, choking, into the temple, Barney in hot pursuit. One of the Bakers walked up to Ahmed and held out his hand. The Book had somehow vanished. Had Ahmed tucked it into his robes?

'Not so fast, my little man,' boomed a familiar voice.

Aunt Hilda, dressed in red Arab pants and an orange turban, stepped around a pillar. Her pistol was pointed straight at the Baker Brother. For a moment he was at a loss and gaped at her, amazed. Trotting behind her was Gaston Champlon, dapper in his solar topee and cream linen suit.

'How did you get here?' I blurted.

'You've led us a merry dance but luckily Gaston here has picked up a few tricks from the trackers.' Aunt Hilda turned to the Bakers. 'As for you, I must confess I'm sorely disappointed in your honesty – ouch!'

There was a popping noise and blood dripped from Aunt Hilda's upraised hand . She stared at it in surprise, as if she didn't understand. Her pistol lay useless where it had fallen in the sand. Ali fired again. Waldo, Ahmed, Rachel and I dropped to the ground as a firestorm of bullets ricocheted around us. Bender Barney, the Brothers, Ali and Gaston all let loose. Raising my head slightly, I could see Champlon was getting the better of it. Even though it was one against four. The little Frenchman was almost dancing as he placed each bullet precisely where it would do maximum damage. His eyes shone with glee. He was shooting to wound not kill, but the others were firing more viciously.

In just a few seconds the battle was over. Blood poured down Barney's leg and his shirt was spattered with gore. One Brother was clutching a wounded arm, all had been disarmed by the hail of Champlon's bullets.

With a shock I realised that Ali was down. He lay crumpled against the wall of the temple, one arm shielding his face, the other still clutching a pistol. At first glance he could merely have been crouching for cover, except blood was smeared on his suit. Then I saw the entrance hole of the bullet, the size and shape of a shilling, it had scorched his white shirt. I was going to accuse Champlon but instead looked at Ahmed. He had acquired a pistol, somehow. Now he dropped it, as if it burnt and turned away, refusing to meet my eye. Meanwhile Champlon was in a fury:

'Go away. Fast like ze wind,' he yelled at the Bakers, waving his pistol. 'You are rotten tomatoes. I was ze fool to ever put a trust in you.'

'Does he mean rotten apples?' Waldo whispered to me. I do not think he had noticed Ali's body. I nodded, unable to speak for the lump in my throat.

'Begone!' Champlon yelled.

The Bakers and Barney were standing quite still, as if waiting for something to rescue them, for their position was quite useless. They were wounded, unarmed, faced with a magician of pistols. I saw one Brother glance at the other. Some private signal, unreadable to the rest of the world, passed between them for without another word they retreated. Barney followed their dark figures, cringing like a whipped dog. Just as they were stepping out of the temple Aunt Hilda let out an explosive noise.

'Haven't you forgotten something, Mr Baker?' she barked.

Both Brothers turned round, like puppets operated by the same string.

'A scarab, about this long,' she held up a stubby thumb. 'Probably in your pocket.'

'It's him.' I said pointing out the Brother furthest away from us. 'He keeps it sewn in the lining of his jacket.'

The man turned his eyes on me, loathing on his papery face: 'You think you're very clever don't you, Miss Salter,' he said flatly.

I shrugged.

'This isn't the end of the game. Not by any means. If I was you, I would be very careful when you return home.'

Aunt Hilda took no notice of his threats. She marched up to Mr Baker and felt first in one side, then the other of his jacket, while he stood motionless. With a swift movement she tore away the jacket's cream silk lining and there it was, a shadow in the flat of her hand. The scarab. A small dark pebble, but precious. For one silent second, both of them gazed at the scarab. Aunt Hilda triumphant. Mr Baker with such longing. He wanted this insignificant-looking thing, wanted it with all he possessed of a heart.

'Don't take it too hard.' Aunt Hilda said turning to Mr Baker, a mocking grin spreading across her face. 'This is just business. I have nothing personal against you,' she paused for a second. 'Well, nothing I could repeat in mixed company.'

The man made a low noise, deep in his throat and then suddenly he spat, aiming straight for my aunt. She clearly couldn't believe the insult, for she froze, outrage in every muscle of her face. The foul gobbet splattered onto her red turban and the Brother turned and stalked off.

'Manners of a skunk!' Aunt Hilda murmured raising her hand to unpeel her turban and shake off the spit. We watched the villains' retreating figures, their cream suits merging into the glare of the sun.

But I had other things on my mind. 'How did you know about the scarab, Aunt Hilda?' I burst out. 'We kept it a secret!'

Aunt Hilda took my arm and patted it, as if she was trying to console me. For once her expression was gentle: 'You were always a rotten liar,' she said.

'That's not true,' I found myself wailing. 'You were *fooled.*'

'Kit, my sweet, did it ever, just once, occur to you that *I* was the one fooling you?'

✏ Epilogue ✏

All of us players in the affair of the scarab were, it seems, entangled in secrets and lies. At one time or another we all wore a mask. Ahmed may have owed his deceptions to concern for his father's health and honour, but others were driven by greed or the longing for fame. I do not wish to judge my aunt too harshly because, despite all her faults, I admire her. She is an inspiration to those young ladies who think a trip to the dressmaker is the height of adventure. Still, we faced a stark choice. Did we let her and her fellow explorer Gaston Champlon into the secret of Ptah Hotep's book? If we did, the Book would be taken away from its homeland to be imprisoned in a distant museum. Furthermore, Ahmed believed that if the Book and scarab were lost, misfortune would haunt his people.

Or did we bury the Book?

In the end it was Ahmed who decided the fate of the Book and the scarab. He traded the scarab with Aunt

Hilda for something far more precious to her; the papyrus cover to Ptah Hotep's manuscripts. This was the object of wonder decorated with magnificent birds, beasts and hieroglyphics which I'd glimpsed in the cave. It was priceless. As my aunt and Champlon promised to donate it to the Pitt Museum, I couldn't help rejoicing. What joy it would bring to my father, whose lifelong obsession with the world's oldest books would here find wonderful scope.

The scarab, the resting place of Ptah Hotep's soul, was secretly buried by Ahmed. Along, of course, with the enchanted thing concealed within that papyrus cover. The World's Oldest Book.

Ahmed felt he had done his duty but sadly for him our adventure did not have a happy ending. He believed it was his bullet that killed Ali, though of course it was impossible to say so for certain, such was the chaos in the temple. Though he despised the man, blamed him for breaking his father's heart, he *was* his cousin. Ahmed was not by nature a killer. By the time we had made the hazardous journey back across the desert to Memphis, Ahmed's father had perished. The funeral rites had already been performed, according to local custom. My friend's grief was unalloyed. The parting from him was painful for us all. Not least, I am guessing, for Rachel who had taken Ahmed under her wing when he was a friendless stray and was now very attached to him.

Maybe some day we would see Ahmed again. Meanwhile Waldo, Isaac, Rachel and I, accompanied by Jabber Jukes, my triumphant aunt and Champlon, sailed back home. Back to Oxford, the land of drizzly afternoons, weak tea and my dreaded governess, 'the Minchin'. I will skirt over the scoldings Waldo got from his anxious mother, the similar lectures Rachel and Isaac received from their guardian. My dear father – who looked as if he hadn't combed his hair the whole time I was in Egypt – was far too dazzled by the cover of Ptah Hotep's book to punish me. To tell you the truth, though adventures are fantastic fun, there is something joyful too, in coming home.

I had my work cut out for me, getting my father to have a bath, soothing Waldo's hysterical mother, sorting out our housekeeping. More importantly I had to find Jabber Jukes an honest job and with Aunt Hilda's help, report what was left of the Velvet Mob to the police. I owed that to the stabbed greener Baruch, to try and seek justice for the shopkeepers of East London. Soon the dazzling sands of Egypt had faded in our minds to the dullness of memory. But there were two gentlemen who were not to escape from Siwa and the cave of the Oracle so easily. I am talking of course of the Baker Brothers.

Were they cursed?

Who knows? Some may regard their misadventures as mere coincidence. What is a matter of fact is that in the following months the Baker Brothers suffered a series of truly sinister accidents. Crossing the Mediterranean their boat was holed and they were lucky to escape with their lives when a passing steamer plucked them off a raft. Back home in Cornwall their castle caught fire and rumours spread that dozens of precious paintings and statues had perished. The next day one of the Brothers contracted an odd skin disease, which covered his flesh with yellow, suppurating sores. The ignorant named this infection the 'mummy bite'. Some say this Baker Brother clings on to life, while others claim he is dead. The ripples of misfortune spread to those who came in contact with the Brothers. Several of their associates are now said to have been infected by the 'mummy bite'.

These days people avoid mention of the Baker Brothers. The smell of the tomb hangs over them. I don't know if they are cursed but I do believe that on that fateful day in Siwa, their greed aroused the displeasure of ancient and powerful forces. Forces that are best left quite alone.

❧ The Maharajah's Monkey ❧

THE NEXT KIT SALTER ADVENTURE

TURN THE PAGE FOR A SNEAK PREVIEW

✑ The Maharajah's Monkey ✑

'There must be something wrong with my eyesight,' Waldo whispered to me as we made our way through the crowd awaiting my aunt's speech. Flustered, after running all the way to the Randolph Hotel, I had no idea what Waldo was talking about. I knew that smirk on his face, though. He thought to embarrass me.

'Surely not,' I replied, in mock sympathy. 'Oh, poor Waldo. Spectacles would spoil your dashing looks.'

'Your aunt. She looks almost . . . handsome!' he grinned. 'Almost like a man dressed as a lady.'

I turned round and scanned Aunt Hilda, dominating her audience from the heights of a massive podium. At first glance she looked like her usual self, a cross between some sturdy heathen statue and a good old British bulldog. At second glance there was something odd. Was that a bow in her hair? That wasn't right. She was wearing a lilac gown with a pretty white lace collar. Too pretty! The lace frothed and tumbled over her dress in a waterfall of feminine frills. I would never wear such a collar. What on earth was my aunt doing in it? Where were her famous check waistcoats? Those pantaloons that confused small children into thinking she was a man?

My gruff, mannish aunt – the woman who had forced the fearsome Tartars of Omsk into giving up the jewelled diadem by sheer willpower – was dressed like the Minchin. Like a flighty young lady dolled up to impress her beau. What on earth was going on?

Then a thought struck me. Champlon. The French explorer must have coaxed my aunt into dressing up like a Gallic poodle. There was definitely something Parisian in the cut of her lilac gown. Monsieur Gaston Champlon was a great dandy, with his waxed moustaches, Malacca canes and embroidered sateen waistcoats. Now he'd turned my aunt into an advertisement for the fashions of the Champs Elysées. Why together, Hilda Salter and Monsieur Gaston Champlon would make a most ridiculous pair of adventurers!

Ignoring Waldo, I settled myself onto a bench. Unfortunately, I knocked into a man in an awful tartan jacket, who scowled at me. Then Waldo stamped on my foot, making me wince in pain.

'Watch out you clumsy oaf!' I snapped, turning on him.

'What have I done?' Waldo replied, good-humouredly, but I was still upset with his remarks about my aunt.

'You stood on my foot. I'm a girl not a Turkey carpet!'

'Oh you're a girl are you? I didn't realise,' his blue eyes tried to gaze into mine, but I looked away. 'If you're a girl,' Waldo went on, 'why don't you behave like one?'

'What, you mean preen and simper and drop my handkerchief,' I retorted. 'No thanks!'

'No one said anything about simpering. Just try and –'

'You'll never be satisfied till I ask your permission every time I want to sneeze!'

In our irritation both of us had raised our voices. I noticed the man in the tartan jacket, a perfect stranger, smirking at our tiff. The man winked at Waldo, as if to signal that girls will be girls. To my astonishment my so-called friend winked right back. This was too much. I turned round, presenting both the evesdropper and Waldo with my back. Studiedly I admired the room. I had never been to this new hotel before and was impressed by the gilt mouldings on the ceiling, the huge plate-glass windows, the ornate chandeliers dripping with glittering crystals. The Randolph was certainly a very modern place, with wonderful views down St Giles of Oxford's ancient butter-coloured colleges. While I was musing thus, I noticed a man, a groom from the look of his coat, scurry up to Aunt Hilda. She pulled out her watch and consulted the time, then with increasing agitation looked down at the notes in front of her. Something was wrong.

I shouldered my way through the crowd to my aunt. She was barking at the groom who'd brought her the message.

'Is everything all right?' I asked.

My aunt turned to me, distraught. 'It's a catastrophe, Kit.'

'What is?'

'The conference was meant to start half an hour ago. Well, I thought Gaston was merely delayed, but Jinks here informs me that his horse has gone. There is no sign of him! He's vanished! You realise what this means!'

'He may have just been called away,' I tried to soothe.

'Poppycock. Monsieur Champlon has played the foulest trick on me.'

'You can't know that, Aunt Hilda.'

'It is as clear as daylight. Gaston Champlon has run out on me, the cowardly cur. I went along with everything, just to please him! He persuaded me into this foolish dress for starters,' her hands plucked at the ruffles on her bodice. 'This is how he repays my trust. This is . . . is too, too awful. For me, Hilda Salter, to be humiliated like this, now, in front of everyone.' Aunt Hilda was no longer bothering to keep her voice low and I saw some of the people in the front row were plainly listening.

'GASTON HAS JILTED ME.'

I wanted to point out to Aunt Hilda that she had been about to form a new Anglo-French exploring team, not become Mrs Champlon, but one look at her face and wiser counsel prevailed. Leaning over the podium I reached out to her. I was surprised, and touched, to feel her hand quivering in mine. Suddenly she felt vulnerable.

'Please, remember your dignity, Aunt Hilda,' I murmured gently. 'People are staring. You don't want this to end up in the newspapers.'

It was the right thing to say. Her hand stiffened inside mine and a stubborn look came into her eyes. 'Certainly not!' she growled. 'I will let no man . . . no Frenchman humiliate me!'

'You must make an announcement,' I went on. 'Think of some excuse.'

She nodded, composing herself. I could see the effort in the lines of strain that stood out on her neck. I left her and hurriedly made my way back through the crowd. Pointedly I ignored my friends' surprised looks. Usually I would have included them in my plans, but today I felt like working alone. As I left the room my aunt had risen and was delivering a speech, hardly a tremble in her bassoon of a voice. With typical bravado she made no mention of the missing Champlon, but forged right into her glorious vision for exploring the Himalayas, the greatest unconquered mountain range in the world. Hilda Salter was going to venture to the roof of the world!

Mid morning and Magdalen Street was relatively quiet. A few people gave me suspicious glances as I ran pell-mell past the golden stones of the new museum – the Ashmolean. I knew my father had organised rooms for Champlon in Jericho; at Worcester College. It was a stroke of luck for I was firm friends with the porter, a man named Simpson. Oxford porters are usually a sullen lot, but my father had a fellowship at Worcester. I had fond memories of playing as an infant in sunlit college grounds.

Simpson was dozing in the Porter's lodge, almost hidden behind a haze of pipe smoke. When I rapped on the window he woke with a start.

'Napping? At ten in the morning?' I asked cheekily.

'You've forgotten your old friends, Miss Kit. What is it? A month since you came to see me? Too grand are you, now you're a fine young lady.'

'I'll never be a fine lady, Simpson,' I retorted. 'Even if I wanted to, it'd be impossible to forget *you* – the lectures you've given me! How is the gout?'

One of the drawbacks of a college porter's job is the amount of fine port and food he is allowed to consume. Simpson paid dearly for his rich diet in shaky knees and chronic indigestion. Indeed I feared that the college would soon retire him.

'Me stomach hurts something dreadful. Feels like I've a bunch of eels in there, it does.'

'You must come round to Park Town. Cook's herbal remedies can cure anything,' I replied and then, the courtesies over, got to the point. 'Simpson, I've come on an errand for Monsieur Champlon. I need to get into his rooms.'

'Right at the back of the college, up three flights of stairs. Me knees won't stand it.'

'Can I have the keys?'

'You're up to some sort of mischief, Miss Kit. I can see it in your eyes,' he grumbled, but nevertheless he trudged over to the keyboard and retrieved a set for me. I took the time to thank him though I was burning to be off. I could feel in my bones that there was some sort of mystery about Champlon's disappearance. Speed was of the essence.

My heart pounding, I raced up the dim and narrow stairwell to Champlon's rooms: 3B on the third landing. The key was a hefty brass affair, which looked like it was made in the middle ages. It was impossible to turn in the lock, I was just about to give up when, with a rending groan, the levers clicked into position and the door creaked open to reveal a large study. The walls were panelled with ancient oak of mellow brown and hung with a number of rugby cups and rowing trophies that I guessed must belong to the student occupant of the room. I could see no sign of Champlon. The room's usual inhabitant struck me as a hearty sort of person who played a lot of sport and didn't trouble himself too much with his lessons. Indeed there wasn't a single book in the study. Then I saw the open door to the bedroom.

Here there was plentiful evidence of the Frenchman in the rows and rows of dandified suits, the lines of polished shoes. There were remarkable quantities of eau de toilette, gold-plated razors, ebony hair and shaving brushes on the dressing table. One of the scent bottles was uncorked, I took a sniff and recoiled in disgust. It was sickly sweet, a combination of musk and jasmine which instantly called Champlon to mind. I knew the Frenchman carried a miniature silver bottle of this awful scent stuff around, I'd seen him take it out and dab some on his wrists. What looked like a brand new full-length mirror had been hung up by the dressing table, probably so that Champlon could check that his attire was faultless. Everything was neatly hung up or lovingly folded and packed away. These were treasured possessions. I found it hard to believe that if the Frenchman had fled, he would have left his beloved things behind.

I sat down on the bed and studied the room, the conviction growing in me that Gaston Champlon hadn't, as my aunt believed, disappeared of his own free will. Something had happened to him. I was guessing it was something sinister, because he was just as excited as Aunt Hilda about their new venture. If their Himalayan expedition was a success, both Aunt Hilda and Champlon stood to make a fortune, not to mention write their names in the history books. There was no way Champlon would have just left Aunt Hilda in the lurch. However, this room was so perfect, so spotlessly clean and tidy it wasn't going to give me any clues.

Or was it?

I shivered in the chill breeze that was blowing through the window. How could I have not it noticed before? On a freezing winter's day the window had been violently thrust upwards – and when I came closer it was clear that a pane of glass, now half hidden by another glass pane, had been smashed. Blending in with the rich reds and browns of the Turkey rug below the window, my eyes were arrested by a series of small muddy marks. I bent down and examined them. They could have been bare footprints, but if so they were made by the smallest of children – no more than a five-year-old. The marks were curiously splayed out, with occasional indentations that must have been made by toe nails. Remarkably long toe nails.

The marks could, I conjectured, have been made by a

young thief, who had smashed the window to gain entrance to Champlon's bedroom. But what a nimble thief! How was it possible to have climbed three storeys up a sheer stone wall?

I leant out of the window. Down below I could make out the cultivated greenery of the college gardens, the glint of boats on the canal and the untamed spaces of Port Meadow beyond. What I had assumed was a sheer stone wall, was, in fact, old and crumbling: plenty of places where an enterprising urchin might grab on to jutting stones. But what made it even more likely that someone had climbed up these walls was the rampant Virginia creeper. The gnarled roots of the flourishing shrub that covered Worcester College's walls were thick enough to support the weight of a child, I was sure of it.

I was glad Rachel was not here. Not to mention my father and all the other people in my life, lining up to tell me how reckless I was. Biting my lip, I eased myself over the windowsill. Moving with extreme caution I found a foothold in the creeper. Then a handhold and then, everso carefully, down I went. You might think I had taken a foolish risk. Believe me I knew what I was doing. I had always enjoyed climbing trees, but I was acutely aware that this time I was not scrumping for apples. If I lost my hold and fell, or the creeper broke, I would be dashed to pieces on the flagstones eighty feet below.

Halfway down the creeper, I became convinced that someone else had made this perilous descent, and very recently too. Fronds of the Virginia creeper were displaced and broken and many of her leaves flattened. Some twenty foot above the ground I saw something white poking out of the creeper's foliage, just past my hand. Straining, I reached out for it and retrieved the thing – a slip of cloth. It was a handkerchief, a dainty piece of the finest white linen. Embroidered in the corner was a monogram of fine curling letters:

G. C. Gaston Champlon

I couldn't help crying out in triumph, causing a student in white cricket flannels who was strolling over the lawn with his nose in a book, to look up in surprise. Luckily whatever he was reading was more interesting than a girl climbing the creeper, for he gave me but a glance. So, I thought, Gaston must have climbed down this creeper. Or, at the very least, someone who had stolen his handkerchief.

The slip of fabric clutched tightly in my hands, I fell down to the ground. The passage of human beings must have left some marks. Nothing, of course, in the flowerbeds under the walls except clods of earth and some withered, wintry stumps of plants. But on the frost-dusted lawn two sets of footprints were visible. The urchin's strange twig-like tracks and following them, at a run by the look of the smudged marks, a set of adult prints. The feet were hurrying away from the college towards the edge of the garden and the canal.

In hot pursuit, I set out after them.